OUR DARLING

OUR DARLING

A NOVEL

D. A. BROCKETT

WESTERN REFLECTIONS
PUBLISHING COMPANY®
Montrose, Colorado

This book is a work of fiction, though based partially on real places, events, and people of 1924 Grand Junction. Unless noted in the final chapter or in the acknowledgements, all names, places, characters, and events are either products of the author's imagination or are used fictitiously. Any other resemblance to actual event locales, or persons living or dead is entirely coincidental.

ISBN 1-890437-89-1
Library of Congress Control Number: 2003112320

First Edition
Printed in the United States of America

Cover and text design by Laurie Goralka Design

Western Reflections Publishing Company®
219 Main Street
Montrose, CO 81401
www.westernreflectionspub.com

Acknowledgements

Yowzah! A novel about the Roaring Twenties can't possibly be written without a lot of help.

First, I'd like to thank my husband, Ben, who constantly validates what I do, pays the bills, tags along for the ride even when he wishes he were golfing. Thanks to my three sons, Jon, Mike and Chris, Chris's wife, Joanie, and my darling granddaughter, Lily. Whether they know it or not, they all challenge me to be the best person I can be.

Second, I must thank Steve Henderson for his astute critiquing and editing. He's even training my sister, and Robbie, you're getting real good. Both Steve and Robbie have encouraged me. Also, a big thanks to my Western Reflections editor, Bonnie Beach, who caught mistakes even I missed.

Others who encouraged me were dear friends: Josh and Annette James, Pastor Gary Buss and his wife, Beth, the Praise Team, Beverly Coney Heirich, Norbert Beilman, Carol Anderson, LuAnn Harrah of Harrah's salon, Cindi Frieling, and Kathy Beshai, who also shared a recent personal moment at her father's graveside. I included, in this book, a pale comparison to the poignancy of her experience.

To many others along the way, thank you all so much.

Next, there are the "teriff" people upon whom I based a couple of my fictional characters. Chris Brown, of Brown's Cycles in downtown Grand Junction, is not only my history buddy, but he is the essence of everything good in Robert Miller. Chris helped me write the parts that pertained to running a bicycle shop, and taught me the history of bicycle shop owners in Grand Junction. Foremost is Porter Carson, whose ancestors still live in Grand Junction and shared some personal photos with me. The customers in Miller Bicycle Shop were right out of Chris's normal day. He is known for helping the "handicapped and hindered" to find mobility on bicycle wheels.

Also of great help was Evan Williamson, grandson to the Treece family from this area. Although hearing impaired, Evan has such a positive outlook on life, you know he's going far. He is a handsome, talented, thoughtful, and classy gent. Evan, thank you, and I wish you all the best. Parts of the real Evan are throughout *Our Darling.*

I want to thank Dalton Trumbo, William Moyer, the late Gesberg family, especially Art and Lillian, and Our Darling, wherever you are.

To all my models, thanks for being the kind of people novels are made of.

Thanks to Kathy Jordan (for so much) and to *The Daily Sentinel.* I couldn't have written this book without you, your articles, or the talented reporters and correspondents who have worked for the *Sentinel* over the past 100 or so years. Gary Harmon, thanks for sharing your interesting day, your insights into the role of a reporter, and for encouraging me. Thanks for introducing me to Bob Thorpe and his wife.

I also appreciate Bobby Alires and his kids for hiking to the cave first and filming it for me, and for being as excited as I was about Our Darling's story. Thanks, Bob Silva, for visiting with me, and Carol Newton, for letting Chris Brown and I wander around the Fair Store. I loved dipping my fingers into the dust of time and rubbing elbows with ghosts. For Dwight at the *Pueblo Lore Magazine,* thanks for putting my ad in your paper. No response, but it was a long time ago. I appreciate it anyway. To Dale Williams, of Abstract & Title, thank you for the time you took to find the patents on the land.

Clint and Janell Dawson, I hope you find what you are looking for. Thanks for the hike to the cave, the ride back and sharing your story with us. God bless.

Karen Armstrong, of the Mesa County Health Department, thanks for your help on behalf of Our Darling.

At the Museum of Western Colorado, Judy Prosser-Armstrong, Sissy Williams, Dave Fishell and Dave Sundal, the Fantastic Four, were so helpful. Thanks for the pictures, stories, memories, leads, and hugs.

Thanks to the Mesa County Public Library, with all its databases of knowledge and helpful librarians. The same goes to the main library in Pueblo, where I found a key piece to my story. Also, I appreciate the Mesa County Clerk and Recorder's Office, and the opportunity to spend hours perusing those lovely, musty ledgers.

Thanks to Jon Austin, Director of the Museum of Funeral Customs in Springfield, Illinois, and to Mike Blackburn of Callahan-Edfast Mortuary, LaNora Trujillo and Paula Maley of Martin Mortuary, and Marilyn Olson, granddaughter of Clyde Martin. Dr. William D. Merkel and his staff, Tonya and Barbara, were very helpful and deserve thanks. Dr. Merkel examined two of my pictures, identifying Lillian by her bone structure. Thanks to Janet Prell, Paulette, Lorrie Ray, Patty Kurtzman, and Lauri Skala, of the Mesa County Sheriff's Office, for your help and encouragement.

I appreciate Reverend Glenn E. Derby of St. Paul's Episcopal Church in Brainerd, Minnesota, for letting me use his *Lonely Ember* story. It truly touched me. Thanks to Will Rogers, whom I quipped several times in the story. My favorite saying is, "No man is great if he thinks he is." This, from a great man.

For those who shared memories, I have to thank Sylvia Baldwin for so many personal remembrances. Thanks to Ruby Roper, Bud and Phyllis Bradbury, Alice Lehman, Mae Coulson, Crafts Black, Georgia Munro, Pat Gormley, and especially Wallace "Bud" Gesberg and Bernice Miller. Thanks to Bob and

Ahna Brock for allowing me to delve into the lives of Wilma
Martin Anderegg Gesberg and her daughter, Betty Brock. Janet
Peyton, thanks for sharing your memories of the Fair, William
Moyer, and of your father, Harry Kissinger, cousin of Mr. Moyer
and longtime manager at the Fair. I enjoyed the old *Sentinel*
papers, too. Michael and Debbie Dunning, thanks for letting me
wander around Harold Gesberg's old home and enjoy the view
into the past.

Karen O'Connor, of Sparrow Perch Studios, thank you for
the beautiful stained glass panel for my cover. Once again, your
insightful talent was just what was needed. For the poem, *Giml*,
thanks to Peggy Godfrey. You open the pages of one's heart with
your lilting words. The inspiring phrase, "Joy is sorrow overcome
and transformed" is taken from *Mountains of Spices*, by Hannah
Hurnard. I recommend that and its prequel, *Hinds Feet on High
Places*. Both books changed my life. Choruses from songs, "Roses
of Picardy" (Frederick E. Weatherley, Haydn Wood 1916),
"Daisy" (Harry Dacre, 1892), and "You're The Cream In My
Coffee" (B. G. DeSylva, Lew Brown, Ray Henderson, 1923) were
included in the book. All are wonderful songs that illustrate the
time they were written.

Many thanks go to my publisher, P. David Smith, of
Western Reflections Publishing, his wife Jan, and their "staff,"
Carole. Thanks for your patience, nudging, expertise and
encouragement.

Special gratitude is saved for the Grandbouche family, who
has found incredible treasure and has lost it, too.

Last of all, thank you dear Lord, for giving me a talent and
a passion to make a difference.

*This book is dedicated to
all those who have lost loved ones
and handled the loss the best way they knew how.*

*In Memory of
Our Darling
And
Jay Grandbouche*

Prologue

"**Y**ou boys are driving me crazy! Summer just started two weeks ago, and you're bored already?"

Charlotte Sterling looked at her sons lounging in front of the sixty-four-inch television set her husband, Ed, had insisted the family "needed."

Josh, age twelve and the oldest of the trio, had one leg dangling over the side of the recliner while the rest of his body bunched in on itself. His hazel eyes were a study of measured disinterest as he watched his brother, Mark, perform some maneuver with his video game controller.

Ten-year-old Mark's body seemed all angles as he fidgeted on the floor, trying to best an appalling creature that looked like a cross between a skeleton and a rhododendron bush.

Carl, the youngest at age eight, kept one eye on the game and half-heartedly flipped through a stack of books at his elbow. Nothing captured his attention for long.

Charlotte sighed at the scene. When she was young, there had never been a moment of boredom. She couldn't understand this generation of children. They had gadgets galore to play with, countless books to read and movies to watch, and — heaven forbid they should step outside — the nearby Gunnison River and its beautiful bluffs just waited to be explored. Yet, her sons were bored! Honestly, Charlotte wondered if the much-touted "Information Age" hadn't ushered in the "Era of Laziness."

She peered at the clock: ten o'clock. Only twelve hours until bedtime. "Mark, when you're done slaying that beast, or whatever the thing is, turn that machine off. I have an idea."

"Not a game of Monopoly again!" muttered Josh.

All three boys groaned. To their surprise, their mother ordered them to get into hiking clothes; she was sending them off for the day and they "had better not come back until sunset." Reluctantly they trudged to their bedrooms, emerging within a few minutes. The boys still felt grumpy.

"Take these and please bring everything back in order, understand?" Charlotte handed each boy an orange life jacket and a backpack. "Josh, you have the essentials."

Josh opened the backpack he was handed and held up its items: canteen, first aid kit, snakebite kit, mosquito spray, sunscreen, liquid blister patches, cell phone, whistle, matches, three pairs of sunglasses, baseball hats, and . . .

"A flare? Mom!"

"One never knows when one will need to signal a rescue plane. I remember when your father and I got stranded on our honeymoon at Lake Powell. If it hadn't been for that fishing boat coming along the next morning, we'd probably still be scrounging for firewood. Thank goodness we had each other to keep warm. What I wouldn't have done to have a flare that night — "

Josh resolutely tossed the flare back into the pack with the rest of the gear.

The brothers surreptitiously rolled their eyes at each other. Their mother worried about everything; from too much salt and fat in their diet, to the slim chance of being kidnapped, to making sure they religiously wore seat belts.

After each received a sack lunch and instructions to avoid canals, dead animals, and sunburn, the brothers sauntered down the driveway. At the road, Carl turned around and waved to his mother.

"You boys be careful!" she called, waving back.

"Right." Mark replied, smiling in as honest a fashion as he could muster.

When their mother shut the door, Josh pushed Carl and Mark. "Come on!"

The boys scrambled behind a nearby tamarisk, where Josh dumped his pack on the ground. They kept the hats, life jackets, and the lunches, consisting of turkey sandwiches, oranges, sunflower seeds, and Oreos.

"Mom likes things tidy, doesn't she?" Mark held up a huge wad of napkins.

All three shook their heads. Their mother just didn't understand the pleasures of grimy fingers. The napkins were plunged back into the depths. Josh pushed the backpack deeper into the bush, then tossed the canteen of water to Mark. When he handed Carl the cell phone, his brothers looked at him curiously. He shrugged.

"You never know . . ."

"Hurry up, you idiot!" Josh complained. "I'm baking here! If you hadn't worn those huge pants, we'd be at the river by now!" Josh ran the back of his hand over his sweaty forehead as heat waves billowed up from the loamy dirt. Trees and brush had disappeared before the boys had crested the bluffs above the canal an hour ago. A dip in the cool river would be more than welcome at that moment.

"Chill, will ya? I'll be done in a minute." Mark was sitting on the spongy ground, gingerly pulling cactus needles out of his wide pant legs. "I couldn't find my shorts, and these old FUBUs were nearest to the door."

"They look moldy. Don't you ever do your laundry?"

"Stick it in your ear!" Mark glared good-naturedly at his brother. "Carl, hand me the canteen, will ya?" Mark pointed to the nearby cactus patch he'd stumbled into. He'd hopped on one foot to safety, but had dropped the canteen. It now rested in the nest of the spiny needles.

Carl looked doubtful. He surveyed the situation from several angles before carefully reaching for the canteen. When he'd snatched it up without mishap, he took an elaborate bow. Josh sighed loudly and stalked toward the bluff's edge. Disgusted, he looked back at his brothers, and then longingly at the undulating river below.

Carl waddled over to Mark and gave him the canteen of water. His pockets were bulging. Mark took a swig of water, then looked at his younger brother.

"You collect any more rocks and your pants are gonna fall down. Why don't ya leave 'em in a pile here and we'll pick 'em up on the way home?"

"Someone might steal them!"

"It's not like they're treasure."

"Who says they're not?" Carl balled his fists up.

"Whatever, squirt. I promise no one will steal your, er, treasure." Mark stood up and swished his hands together as Carl unloaded his booty. "Been looking for anything in particular?"

"Fossilized dinosaur bones."

Mark's face was bland. "I'd settle for a few Indian arrowheads. Easier to carry."

After Carl had deposited his rocks in a neat pile, he joined Mark and Josh. He peeked back at his treasure and hoped his brother was right. The threesome descended the rocky slope.

Upon arrival, they dropped all but their underwear near the railroad tracks by the riverbank. An argument ignited when Carl insisted they wear their life jackets. His brothers disagreed, but when Carl refused to go into the water if they didn't, they put theirs on, griping loudly.

The crisp water stung their toes for a second, and then the air filled with jubilant war whoops. For an hour they splashed, swam, and looked for frogs in the river. Once, a train thundered by, and they watched, enthralled. Even though they sat on the bank across from the tracks, the ground beneath them trembled. They waved enthusiastically, and the conductor returned their greetings with a wide grin. Soon after, they swam across the river to their belongings.

"Anyone getting hungry?" Josh reached for his shirt. Even in the sunshine, goose bumps formed on his damp limbs.

"I'm up for it. Hey, our cave! Let's have lunch there." Mark pointed at a long outcropping of rocks a couple of hundred feet away. Near the top, the dark entrance of a cave invited the boys in.

Carl's stomach was feeling decidedly empty. He calculated the minutes it would take to climb the boulders to the cave and hurried to dress. He was thankful his pockets were empty as he stood up before his brothers did. He'd be the first there. For once.

"Wait up, squirt. I've got your lunch." Mark was within reach and grabbed Carl's ankle.

"Let go of me — hey, cool!" Carl's whine turned to awe as he pointed upward. Two *F/A-18 Hornets* slit the clear cobalt curtain, seeming to chase one another. They reached the southwest sky in moments pursued by the roar of their engines, which deafened the air around the boys.

"I can't wait to fly one of those babies when I join the Navy!" exclaimed Josh.

"Navy pilots fly the *F/A-18E Super Hornets*, Josh." Carl sat down to oust a pebble from his tennis shoe.

"Oh, what do you know, anyway?" Josh climbed over a boulder at the base of the rock outcropping. Mark shook his head at Carl and followed his older brother.

"The McDonnell Douglas *F/A-18 Hornet* is a direct descendant of the Northrop Cobra. Its wingspan is thirty-seven feet, five inches, and it is fifty-six feet long. It can go more than 1,360 miles per hour. But the Super Hornet has longer range, an aerial refueling capability, and improved carrier suitability. They are bigger, faster, and they kick butt! Then again," Carl conceded, "the Blue Angels fly Hornets."

Josh and Mark stopped mid-climb and stared down at Carl. Then they stared at each other. "Damn!" they said in unison.

Carl cocked his head to one side and grinned.

"*Come on, squirt. I'm hungry.*" Mark lent a hand to his little brother and the trio picked their way over bigger and bigger boulders until they stood at the mouth of the cave.

The cave was little more than a niche carved over the centuries by the wind along the river. It was just deep enough, about fifteen feet, for the three boys to spread out comfortably. In the middle of the cave floor was a two-foot high rectangular rock that they had always used for a table. From the cave's entrance, the remnants of an abandoned coal mine, burrowed directly into the cliff side across the river bend, could be seen. The rock beneath the opening was stained black, is if coal had been dropped to the railroad tracks below.

"*I wonder who worked that mine. Looks ancient,*" Mark asked as he handed Carl his lunch. He held up Carl's cookies and pretended to keep them for himself. Carl hit his brother on the arm. "*Okay, okay. Can't you take a joke?*" Mark feigned pain.

Carl opened his Oreos first and stuffed a whole one in his mouth. He chewed thoughtfully. "*There were hundreds of coal mines around here, after Grand Junction was founded in 1881. The biggest mining operation was the Little Bookcliff, at the base of the Bookcliff Mountains. It was one of the first and had its own railroad to town. Another biggie was the Halegonian Mine at the top of the Fifth Street Bridge.*"

"*Could you be any geekier?*" Josh crossed his eyes and wobbled his head.

Carl ignored him. "*Last week of school, our class took a historical tour with Dave Fishell. Interesting man.*"

"*Bet he couldn't tell us what those rock foundations are that we passed on the way up.*"

"*Those are interesting, aren't they?*"

Josh guffawed. "*Not! Do you think we could forget the history lesson and just eat?*"

For a few minutes, the cave was filled with appreciative munching. Josh finished his lunch first and gathered his trash. As soon as he stuffed it into his pocket he was ready to leave. "*Aren't you guys done yet?*"

"*Could you be more impatient?*" Carl tossed the last bite of his sandwich in his mouth.

While waiting, Josh picked up a small stone and heaved it at the rectangular rock in the center of the cave — their table. The action produced a loud thunk. The three brothers stared at each other for a moment.

"*That sounded hollow!*" Josh scrambled to his knees.

Mark picked up the stone Josh had thrown and threw it again. Another thunk. "*This isn't a rock at all!*" He picked at the chink the stone had made. "*It's more like dried mud, and* — *there's something underneath it!*"

"*Buried treasure!*" Carl's eyes lit up.

Mark threw the stone down and looked around. "*We need something sharper. Run down to the tracks, Josh, and bring us a spike.*"

"*Do I look like your errand boy?*"

"*Just do it!*"

Josh crossed his arms and didn't budge.

Mark rolled his eyes. "*All right, but don't start without me.*" As he passed Carl, he ruffled his brother's tawny hair. "*No offense, squirt, but I sure hope this is something better than a dinosaur bone.*"

"*You were right, Carl!*"

The cave was a mess. The mysterious object had been hacked at with a railroad spike until a wooden box had finally been revealed. A slatted lid was nailed tightly on top, and between the slats, a white chest could be seen.

Josh stepped forward. Grabbing hold of the first slat, he pulled with all his strength, grimacing with the effort. It creaked and groaned and finally cracked. He did the same with the other slats. Pretty soon, the chest lay exposed, covered in powdered clay.

Solemnly, Josh lifted it and laid it on the ground. He looked at his youngest brother. "Carl, you get the honor of opening it."

The youngest boy eyeballed the chest. He got a funny feeling in his gut, like maybe, they weren't supposed to be doing this. With trembling fingers he touched the chest. "It feels warm!"

The brothers froze, eyes widening.

"Aw, go on." *Josh scooted back an inch.* "It's summer, remember?"

Carl needed courage. He crossed his fingers and whispered, "Buried treasure, buried treasure, buried treasure." *Gripping the lid with both hands, he closed his eyes. The lid slid off easily, a gush of sour air escaping its prison.*

"Ew!" *Carl said.*

"What the — ?" *Josh said.*

"Damn!" *Mark said.*

Nestled on soft folds of aged muslin lay a tiny mummified baby.

All three sat back on their heels, amazed. Josh picked up the lid and saw a metal plate, covered in a dark gray patina. Perhaps it held an answer. With his shirt, he rubbed it until he was able to see the inscription. It read: "Our Darling."

"Our Darling? Who's that?"

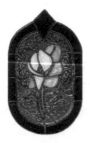

Chapter One

It was a typical afternoon on Main Street in Grand Junction. Tired mothers dragged tired children, pushing tiny children in tiny perambulators, while old men told old stories on street corners. Shoppers, their arms full of purchases, bustled from busy shop to busy shop, and important businessmen hurried to important business meetings.

Oak Miller wove his way through the crowd. Methodically, he pulled a newspaper out of his shoulder bag, folded it with one hand, and dropped it at the doorway of each business.

Nearly everyone subscribed to *The Daily Sentinel*. It was rumored the *Sentinel* was buying the struggling *Grand Junction News*, but Oak knew the rumors were true. Talk around work was that the deal would go through in a couple of days.

He was proud he worked for the only newspaper that had survived the forty-three years Grand Junction had been a town. He just wished he were more than a simple newsboy.

His route had started on the north side of Main Street, at Lilja Dodge next to the *Sentinel* building. He'd just crossed to the south side at Seventh and Main when he heard a loud *ah-oo-gah* close behind him. He shot up on the sidewalk.

Dugger Snyder had one of the plainest faces the world had ever seen. His bulbous nose was the first thing Oak always noticed. It was underlined by a slitted mouth, and above his nose, dark scoundrel eyes looked down on the world. Ugliness hadn't gotten in the way of the high school junior's life, though. He had arrogance and money, which gained him friends, status, and a brand new Ford Model T coupe. Hal and Chas, Dugger's cronies, grinned as the vehicle barely missed Oak's heel.

"There are only two kinds of pedestrians, Miller. The quick and the dead!" Dugger tossed his taunt out the side window as he passed.

And there are three kinds of drivers: the good, the bad, and the ugly. And you're the last two. Oak snickered. He wished he had the courage to say that to Dugger's face.

As the coupe continued down the street, Oak heard intermittent honks followed by shrieks and curses. *One of these days, that knucklehead is going to have an accident, and it won't be pretty.*

Located on the southwest corner of Seventh and Main, the Avalon was a year old and one of the most beautiful buildings in Grand Junction. It was managed by *The Daily Sentinel*'s publisher, Walter Walker, who brought in vaudeville acts, Chautauquas, opera stars, speakers, and plays, as well as the finest movies in town. It was also where the Grand Junction High School Class of 1924 had held their graduation ceremony that week.

The tall windows reflected the early June sky, which hung close to the ground, pregnant with rain. Musical instruments squawked loudly, even though the Avalon's glass doors were shut against the unusually gray day. Normally, the orchestra played the musical scores for the Avalon's movies, but today they were warming up for the evening's special entertainment.

Oak stopped to read a colorful poster in front of the theater. "The Passing Show," praised as "a cascade of song, a downpour of talent, and a Niagara of beauty," was there for one "simply stupendous" night. *Sounds all wet to me,* thought Oak as he continued on his route. *Like this eternal spring.*

He tossed a paper at Art's Tire Shop and waved to the owner, Art Gesberg. His amiable face framed sad eyes. He'd lost his young wife, Ruth, to scarlet fever a few years back, but was remarried to a nice enough lady, Lillian. She worked at the Fair Store with Oak's mother, Eulila.

Oak halted in mid-stride. Across the street, Dalton Trumbo was heading toward the *Sentinel*, his thin trench coat flapping behind him. Oak wondered, with a tinge of envy, what great story he was working on that day.

Dalton had the tendency to barrel along like he was late for a train; his head always entered a room before the rest of his slight body. His baby face belied his intelligence, but his eyes did not. They flicked about restlessly, reflecting worldliness beyond his years. He was cynical with a wry sense of humor, pugnacious, generous to a fault, yet when he spoke, it was with eloquence and style.

Both young men had just graduated but, unlike Oak, Dalton was heading to college this fall. The Millers didn't have enough money to send Oak. He'd have to find another way to get to New York, where he wanted to be a crack reporter for the *Times*.

Oak had followed Dalton's accomplishments since they were freshmen. Excelling at nearly everything, Dalton had been president of the graduating class, president of the Boosters Club, star of the high school debating team, and worked on the award-winning *Orange and Black* school newspaper. He was a correspondent for a couple of Denver newspapers, as well as a reporter for *The Daily Sentinel*. Oak wanted to be just like him. *Not likely, chum.*

Oak called out and waved, half hoping Dalton would return it. For once. Dalton gave Oak a quizzical look before the *Sentinel* door shut behind him.

Ain't that the bee's knees! Oak pulled a newspaper out of his bag and folded it. *Least he looked my way!*

With keen interest, Oak had gathered details regarding the Trumbos, who lived in a small house a block away from the Millers, on Gunnison Avenue. Dalton's father, Orus, worked as a salesman for Bert Benge, the Shoe Man. It was the latest in a string of short-lived jobs. He seemed intelligent and capable, yet the man simply couldn't stay employed.

Orus had a vegetable garden that rivaled even Robert Miller's, Oak's father. For years, Dalton had sold those vegetables around town, and they were said to be of the highest quality.

Oak didn't know Dalton's mother's name; he'd only seen her in her yard, digging in the flower beds or hanging up clothes. Dalton was the only son, but he had two younger sisters. The oldest girl, Elizabeth, was the first child to enter the pool at Moyer Natatorium on Opening Day in 1922.

The Trumbos were Christian Scientists. Dalton had taken a razzing by his junior peers when he handed the school nurse a note from his parents excusing him from getting a diphtheria vaccine. The rest of the students had been lined up, sniggering behind their hands, but Dalton had held his chin up as he walked back to the empty classroom. That took guts, and Oak's awe of the man grew. By the time Dalton had graduated, so had everyone else's. "That young man is going places," they'd exclaimed.

Oak believed it — and wholeheartedly wished it was him they gushed over.

A cool breeze kicked up momentarily, and Oak pulled his jacket collar closer. An old newspaper flapped down the sidewalk, coming to rest on the concrete street next to the curb. Oak reached down and stuffed it into his pocket. He liked a clean town.

Next to Art's Tire Shop was Miller Bicycle Shop. When he entered the establishment, Oak's father was waiting on a customer, a matronly, middle-aged woman who spoke in exclamation points.

The odor of rubber assaulted Oak's nostrils, but he acclimated to it quickly. He dropped his heavy newspaper bag by the door and sidled past his father to the back of the shop. Along the aisle sat neat rows of Excelsior and Henderson bicycles made by Arnold, Schwinn & Co., as well as bicycles by Harley Davidson. One concrete wall sported accessories, which included a variety of tires and tubes, bicycle lamps, and even toolboxes.

Evan Treece was working on a custom bicycle. The area around him was littered with used bicycles in different stages of repair. Most of the tires were mud-encrusted, dusting the grease-stained floor with geometric dirt clods as they'd dried and fallen off. Wooden-handled screwdrivers, a monkey wrench, a wheel-truing jig, a ball peen hammer, and a tire mouse, used to patch tires, rested on the nearby bench.

Leaning into his current project, Evan worked the large metal vise mounted to a heavy wood workbench. His dress suit was encased in a canvas overall, and a long apron covered that. The pockets strained with unidentified contents.

Oak pulled out the old newspaper he'd captured and tossed it into the trash bin by the back door.

"Hey, Evan, everything jake?"

"Don't have time to beat my guns, Oak. On deadline, as you'd say."

"That's *gums*."

"Eh?"

"Beat my *gums*, not 'guns.'"

"Tell it to Sweetheart."

It's Sweeney. Oak didn't have the heart to correct Evan. The man was intent on keeping up with current slang, but by the time his child, who wouldn't be born for another two months, was a teenager, the slang would have changed. *Some people's fathers.*

Evan wiped his hands on his apron and held out a calloused hand. "I guess I could use a tiny break."

Oak shook his hand. "Little one almost here?"

Evan pooched out his flat belly, indicating late-stage pregnancy with his hands. "A couple more months. Can't wait. May I help you?"

"Naw. Need to speak to Father. Need to borrow the auto tonight. Junior-Senior Banquet."

"Congratulations."

Oak nodded. He watched the shop cat, Slugged, who'd been napping in the back corner, awaken and stretch. He immediately fell out of his box with a thud, but righted himself. Amused, the two men watched the chunky calico carefully pick his way along the aisle to the front of the shop. His gait was disjointed, like a marionette's.

As a kitten, the Millers had named him Slugger. His mottled fur and brutish face made him look like a thug, though his manner was gentle as a dove's. Last summer he'd been hit by a wayward baseball as he chased a rival cat through Washington Park, near the Miller's home. Twenty dusty, sweaty kids piled around his unconscious body and held their breath. Within moments the cat had come round, and everyone exhaled in relief. This was followed by another gasp: Slugger's eyes had crossed.

Since then, the feline walked into walls, misgauged heights, and frequently jumped right when he meant to jump straight. Robert had brought him to the shop to live, where it was safer for the poor creature. Oak, who'd felt a kinship with the misfit since he, himself, had been dropped on his head at birth, renamed the cat Slugged.

Oak waved to Evan and followed the cat to the front, reaching down and tugging on a furry ear. It twitched.

"Now, I'll be back next week to pick up my grandniece's birthday present, Mr. Miller, so don't disappoint me! Oh! What an adorable little kitty!" The woman drew out the word "adorable" and added a musical note. Numerous bracelets clanked to her wrist as she reached down to pet Slugged. He looked lovingly up at her, rubbing against her ring-bedecked fingers.

"Why, his eyes! What haaappened to the dear?"

"It's a long story, Mrs. Crow," Robert Miller said, clearly weary of the woman's presence.

But, Slugged was clearly enjoying it. With a chirp, he reared to jump on the counter next to the woman.

"Well, aren't you the sweetest — eek!"

Missing his mark, Slugged landed in the center of the woman's ample bosom, clinging tenaciously to gingham and organdie. Mrs. Crow swung him back and forth in an attempt to dislodge him, her long string of beads whacking Robert mercilessly as he tried to pry Slugged off without offending the woman's propriety.

"If you'd hold still, ma'am," Oak's father said.

The shop filled with tiny screams, until Slugged finally dropped of his own volition to the floor and sauntered away.

"Well, I never!" Mrs. Crow huffed to the door.

"We'll — we'll see you next week?" Robert called hesitatingly after her. "Ma'am?" Along his right temple, a purple vein began to throb.

The bell over the door trembled discordantly. The moment the door closed, Oak burst into laughter.

His father turned to him and squinted. "Was there something you were wanting, young man?"

Oak was immediately sober. His father never raised his voice, but Oak always felt as though he'd been yelled at. He cleared his throat. "Sir, may I borrow, um — "

Robert hobbled over to the counter and hitched his left pant leg up until the wooden peg was exposed. Unconsciously, he scratched the wood near where his ankle would have been. "Get to the point, Oak. I'm busy."

Sergeant Robert Miller had left a part of his leg in Europe during the Great War, but he'd brought back a sizeable chip on his shoulder to replace it. Six years had passed since he'd come home wounded, and every day since, that purple vein made an appearance.

Fidgeting with the buckle on his bag, Oak said, "See, sir, tonight's the banquet, at Margery Hall. I was hoping I could borrow, er, the Ford?"

Oak was disgusted with himself. He hadn't meant to end on a question mark. He'd wanted to sound assured and grown-up, like a high school graduate should sound. Damn the man! He could reduce a giant to an ant.

"No."

"But sir!"

"But me no buts, Oak. I have work for you to do in the vegetable garden. There will be no entertainment for you until the weeding is done." Robert picked up a stack of receipts and squared their corners.

Unsure of whether to push the subject, Oak looked back at Evan, who shook his head slightly.

"I'm heading to the accountant, Evan. Hold down the shop." Robert waved the receipts at his helper, walking past his son as if he wasn't there.

"Don't be too hard on him," said Evan.

Oak walked back to Evan. He could feel the heat in his cheeks. It embarrassed him that there had been a witness to his father's dressing down. "What's that supposed to mean?" he asked.

"He really cares about you."

Says you, buddy! "Funny way of showing it, Evan."

"He's been through a lot — "

"So Father lost a leg; life goes on." Oak felt uncomfortable at the derision in his own voice, but his father deserved it!

"The Great War robbed him of more than his leg, Oak. Robert also lost his innocence and his identity." Evan paused. "Your father came home, but he hasn't stopped fighting. He brought the enemy with him."

"What enemy?" Oak swept his arms around wildly. "I don't see an enemy. Don't make excuses for him, Evan!"

"Have some compassion. And some patience. This war won't be won quickly."

"It's been six years! Looks to me like this 'enemy' you speak of, Evan, has already won."

"He's your father, Oak."

"Huh! Such as he is."

"If that's what you really think, then you've not looked deep enough, to the real man."

"I've wasted my life trying to see the 'real' Robert Miller. All I see is a mean and selfish man."

"You're misjudging him, I tell you."

"I'm not misjudging anything," Oak called over his shoulder. He reached the front door and turned. "You have no idea what it's like living with him, Evan." He hefted his newspaper bag onto his shoulder. It seemed much heavier.

As Oak crossed Sixth Street, the clouds let loose, drenching him in cold rain.

Perfect, Oak grumbled.

Shoppers scrambled to get under the striped awnings shading most store entrances. Oak didn't have that luxury. He pulled down his serge cap, hurrying past the vacant brick building that had originally been an opera house and later, the courthouse. An elegant replacement for the courthouse had been built a block away and was just dedicated. Rivulets of rain drained down the sidewalks to the street. Oak sloshed through them, soaking his cuffed trousers and oxfords.

Next to the old courthouse, the newly appointed police chief, Bert Watson, stood under the dripping awning at the entrance of Your Cafeteria. Bert's signature Stetson brushed the edge of the low awning. There was an ordinance being discussed to raise all the awnings downtown. Oak's five-foot, eight-inch frame never suffered the inconvenience of Bert's lanky six feet.

Arms akimbo, the chief somberly surveyed the crowded Interurban trolley clanging along its glistening rails toward the east end of Main. Its evening trek through the downtown area would pick up office workers and other employees, as well as shoppers, carrying them home as far away as Fruita. For those traveling that distance, the Interurban changed a three-hour horse and buggy trip from Grand Junction into a forty-five minute pleasure ride.

"Afternoon, Miller. Everything all right?" Bert Watson made a point to know everyone's name and business. He was friendly, but Oak knew the man wouldn't hesitate to make an arrest, even if he'd played cards with you the night before.

"Everything's jake, Chief." *Nothing a good tar and feathering wouldn't solve,* he thought, slapping a newspaper into Bert's hand. "This one's on me," he said ungraciously.

"Kind of you, Oak," he remarked, tucking the paper under his arm.

At the moment, Oak didn't feel like pretending he was flattered. As police chief, Bert enjoyed many favors from townspeople and businesses. It came with the territory, and it was expected.

"Say, something smells good," Oak said, his bad mood lightening a little as the spicy aroma of Your Cafeteria's Blue Plate Special, roast meatloaf, wafted from the open doorway into the moist afternoon. He inhaled deeply. Stomach rumbling, he decided a strawberry malted would ease his hunger and help him forget his father. He'd stop at Mesa Drug after deliveries.

He cruised by downtown window displays, a panorama of automobile parts, bicycle tires, toys, hardware, fashions, and furniture; all artistically arranged to draw the eye and beckon the buyer.

Oak rarely caught a glimpse of himself, but he was used to blending into the background, with his field mouse coloring. Of average height and weight, his unremarkable eyes, nondescript nose, and minimal mouth melded into a forgettable face. He'd been in first grade when he discovered his obscurity. He was always the last to be picked for a game, if not completely overlooked. In class, his raised hand was passed over for a more frantic one, and even slicking back his brown hair with pomade, the latest hairstyle, had won him no popularity contests.

A part of Oak felt obligated to his destiny. Why fight what God had given — or not given — him? Maybe, he could work with it.

In second grade, when he learned to write, his world opened up. It may not be in the looks department that he shined, but when Oak set pencil to paper, another destiny emerged, one that offered great possibilities.

That's why he wanted to go to New York. He had a good face for a reporter. Stylishly written articles would be his calling card, and when he made a name for himself, *everyone* would notice him! Including Lazuli Waters.

Especially the lovely Lazuli.

The door leading upstairs to Margery Hall was open, and as Oak tossed a paper on the step, he peeked upward. This was where the Junior-Senior Banquet would be held tonight. The wide wooden stairs were scratched and worn from years of feet tramping up to the second floor dance hall. A landing at the top of the stairs spread itself out before the hall's entrance and wound its way to the right where a hallway had indoor restrooms.

It was tradition for the junior class to honor the graduates each June. The Class of 1924 would be sent off with a four-course meal, gifts bestowed by faculty, toasts, and readings. A lively dance would finish off the evening.

"Excuse me, please."

Oak held the door wider so a pretty girl, arms loaded with cherry and silver-gray bunting, the colors of the senior class, could squeeze past him. Without a backward look, she started up the stairs, an air of importance defining her mincing steps. With appreciation he watched the ascension, her boyish dress swirling around attractive calves.

Yowzah! How he loved the new flapper craze!

Unconsciously, he began to dictate an article:

The Stars Weren't The Only Things Shining Last Night
By Oak Miller
Dateline: June 7, Grand Junction

In what was surely the most vivid display of finery exemplifying the "Modern" movement ever seen on the high desert, young ladies from the junior and senior classes of Grand Junction High School descended upon Margery Hall last night. Most sported the smart and stylish "bobs" and "flapper" dresses. Oh yes, there were a few fellas and faculty there, too.

*Honored were the 1924 graduates, who remi-
nisced their triumphs, tragedies, and shenanigans
enjoyed during their "salad" school days.*

*After the delicious meal, The Brown Orchestra
provided the evening's music . . .*

Oak continued to dictate his article as he turned into the bright interior of the Fair Store, which graced the southeast corner of Main and Fifth Streets.

The owner of the Fair, William Moyer, was Grand Junction's hero. Any problem brought to the diminutive man was solved quickly. The destitute found a handout, the forlorn found comforting words, the widowed and divorced found a job. Businessmen counted on his apt advice and deep pockets. Routinely, distraught mothers dragged wayward children to "Uncle Billy" for a friendly little chat. Since a piece of penny candy followed the lecture, rarely was a visit unprofitable.

Everyone knew Mr. Moyer cared deeply about the welfare of his town.

One of his greatest acts of benevolence came after a schoolmate of Oak's drowned in the Colorado River, then the Grand River, in 1921. Mr. Moyer immediately had a natatorium built and then donated it to the city of Grand Junction the following June. He stipulated there would always be two free days a week for the children, which he hoped would stop the rash of drownings in unsafe waters.

When the glass doors of the Fair whooshed closed behind him, Oak felt transported to a New York or Paris department store. Everything new and imaginative was sold within the Fair's walls.

Mr. Moyer had made it the finest department store between Denver and Salt Lake City. Rich mahogany accents, potted palms, tables of neatly folded merchandise and clever display signs invited one to stay and shop awhile. Harold Woolverton and his brother, Bernhard, were window dresser and arranger of display tables, respectively. They were exceptional at what they did. Harold's window displays had even won several national awards.

Though the main floor bustled with customers and clerks, people spoke softly, almost reverently. This floor held men's and boy's fashions, jewelry, handkerchiefs, and notions. The basement included hardware, toys, bathroom fixtures, and china, while upstairs, women's fashions and public restrooms were found.

When Oak's mother started working at the store in 1921, women's fashions were just beginning to change. Back then, the older ladies wore drab wool and cotton dresses that barely revealed their ankles. In a few short years, the newest styles had happily moved to colors such as Copenhagen blue, wild honey, bright red, almond green, fawn, and oakwood brown. Fabrics included "Pamico" cloth, Canton and silk georgette crepe, voile, gingham, and silk.

Men's fashions moved from knickerbockers, or "knickers," to suits with striped or colored shirts of putty, peach, blue-gray, biscuit, and cedar.

Oak climbed the stairs to the first floor mezzanine. Usually Mrs. Ullery was visible as she worked the "bank," a system of pulleys and canisters that came directly from the department clerks. Mrs. Ullery would check the sales receipt for mistakes, count the money and make change if necessary, then send the canister back to its department.

No one was sitting at the desk, so Oak knocked on the office door.

Once in a while Mr. Moyer was in, but usually he walked the floor visiting with shoppers, or he was across the street at the Grand Valley National Bank, where he was Chairman of the Board.

When Belle Lay, Mr. Moyer's longtime office manager and friend, was alive, Moyer had spent more time in the office.

Miss Lay had died the year before, unexpectedly; since then, Moyer seemed to avoid his office unless to advise a colleague or speak privately with a friend. It was rumored that he and Miss Lay had been acquainted on a more intimate level than friendship, but Oak refused to believe it. The man was married, after all.

"I'll be with you in a moment," came a cordial voice on the other side of the door. He could hear the clatter of an adding machine.

While Oak waited for the door to open, he read a notice hanging eye level on the wall:

> *The Ideal Service Club of the Fair Store will have their regular monthly meeting this evening. There will be election of officers, and each member has been asked to submit the best article on salesmanship they have been able to find. Prizes are to be awarded to the persons handing in the best ones. The meeting will close with refreshments.*

Oak's mother, who worked in Women's Ready-to-Wear, said Mr. Moyer was always promoting progressive ways of selling. He believed the customers should be treated with the utmost respect, but often they didn't know what they really wanted. The Fair salespeople were trained to gently "guide" the customer in making the right choice.

The office door finally opened and Mrs. Ullery, a petite woman whose dark eyes twinkled behind round glasses, appeared. Oak greeted her and then laid twenty papers neatly inside the door, on the polished wood floor. Each employee would take a copy home that night. Oak wished the woman a good day, then went in search of his mother.

Eulila Miller was standing outside a dressing room, gently speaking with a woman on the other side of the door. "Ma'am, I'm afraid we are out of size eight. Perhaps a twelve? I'm sure you'll be more comfortable. Here is an ever-so-lovely Fancy Figured Silk Mixed Crepe. From New York! It's sure to flatter your figure." There was a tinge of hysteria in her voice.

"Noooo, thank you! It's either a size eight or nothing at aaaall!"

"I will do my best, ma'am." Eulila turned away with an exasperated sigh. When she saw her son, she walked over to him.

"Honestly, even a size twelve is tight. An eight! Some people just can't see themselves for what they really are," she whispered as she hurried by Oak. "I'll be with you soon, my dear."

Amused, Oak looked around. He was disappointed that Lazuli was nowhere to be seen. He wandered to the restroom, and when he returned, his mother's customer was gone. She was hanging up several dresses that needed to be turned inside out.

"My land, there's a tear!"

"Mother, may I speak with you?"

"Where's my kiss, son?" She offered her cheek to Oak, who checked to see that no one was looking before obliging his mother. "Thank you, dear. Now what is the problem?"

"Father won't let me take the auto to the banquet tonight unless I work in the garden first. Mother, he's impossible! I'll miss the dinner altogether."

Eulila put her fingers to her smile and tapped it. "My dear, the world is not falling apart," she said. "Attend your festivities. If there's any trouble, I'll talk to your father. Now go see Harry Kissinger in Men's. Tell him to set you up in a nice suit."

Somehow, Oak's mother always made things right. He felt a rush of affection and, without prompting, gave her another kiss on the cheek.

"Aren't I the lucky one?" she said, pushing Oak in the direction of the elevator.

Kissinger, the manager of Men's Wear, held his hands in front of him while talking to John Gesberg, the longtime manager of Hardware. A first cousin of Mr. Moyer, Kissinger was much younger than Gesberg and a bit taller, with dark, side-swept hair, and a formal demeanor. Oak didn't know him very well, but he was well acquainted with Gesberg.

All the Fair employees went to his farm on Orchard Mesa every March for a picnic.

In his late fifties, John Gesberg was still a handsome man. His hair had silvered and was combed to the side. A thick handlebar mustache enveloped his mouth and blue-green eyes sparkled with brimming humor. One always got the impression he was enjoying a private joke.

He was physically fit, mainly because he had an aversion to automobiles. His son, Art, who owned the automobile tire shop, had given his parents a Ford Model T, and the first and only time John had driven the vehicle, it, and his ego, wound up in a ditch. Since then, he walked or rode a bicycle the few miles from Orchard Mesa to work every day. On Sundays, his wife, Agnes, chauffeured them to church.

Though distrustful of the automobile, John Gesberg was a progressive man. He'd worked for the Fair twenty years, and whether Mr. Moyer had rubbed off on Gesberg or vice versa, these two men thought alike. Not only did he take delight in any new-fangled thingamajig that came along, he would "improve" upon it. At gatherings the Gesberg sons, Harold, Leslie, Carl, and Art, often told hilarious stories of growing up with their father's inventions.

One story that brought universal groans involved an enema "machine" their father created after he'd read purgatives were good for a body's constitution. Once a week the boys were thrust on "Purgatory" and subjected to a thorough cleansing. John didn't understand why they couldn't appreciate its wonderful benefits, but he let the boys off the hook when they all four folded their arms and refused to use it any more. Leslie had once joked that that machine was why Harold was the only brother to father a child.

In spite of the failures, the Gesbergs enjoyed many "firsts" because of John's ingenuity. They were the first family to have running water on Orchard Mesa. After John built their large concrete block house, he put a tank in the attic and filled it with artesian water from the natural well near the cemetery. Gravity brought the water to the sinks and shower.

When they moved to the property overlooking the Gunnison River, theirs was the first farmhouse to have electricity. The generator made a lot of noise, but the Gesberg family didn't mind. It was the sweet sound of progress and, to them, as natural as the croaking frogs and cheeping crickets.

"Hello, young man. What can I help you find?"

Harry Kissinger had said goodbye to John Gesberg, who touched his brow to both men and whistled his way downstairs. Kissinger turned his attention to Oak.

"Mother sent me over for a suit. For tonight."

"Ah, yes, the final fling before you youngsters have to think seriously about life. Eat, drink, and be merry, for tomorrow you — well, never mind. Just enjoy yourself this week." Kissinger led Oak to a rack of ready-made suits. "Will you be going to college?"

"Not sure yet, Mr. Kissinger. Funds may be a problem. Thought I'd work and save some simoleons."

Kissinger nodded. It wasn't his way to pry, but he'd ask William about Oak. Only a few people knew that his cousin had helped many deserving young men through college, anonymously. William had asked him to keep his eyes open. Perhaps he would help Oak.

"What do you think of this?" Kissinger held up a tan suit. "Kirschbaum Warm Weather Weaves are tailored with great skill. Accompanied by a straw hat, the new striped shirt, and a bowtie, you'll be as natty as they come."

Oak tried it on, liking what he saw, but his spirits deflated when he read the price tag. "Have to talk to Mother. Be right back."

In his stocking feet, he rode the elevator to Women's Ready-to-Wear. Two things stopped Oak in his tracks as he debarked the elevator.

The first was his mother stuffing her thick bun up under a red cloche hat. She turned her head to the side, checking her profile in the mirror, and then tittered like a schoolgirl.

Instinctively, Oak looked around to make sure his father wasn't nearby. He wasn't a "Modern" by any stretch of the imagination. He'd hate his wife even looking at a flapper hat.

"Eulila, it takes twenty years off your age!"

"Why, that would make me *six*, Lazuli."

"You don't say?" This elicited a comradely grin from both ladies.

Oak stood transfixed. To him, Lazuli Waters was the most beautiful creature on earth. He'd thought so ever since Frosh Latin, when he'd sat next to the new girl in town.

To acquaint the teacher with their names, she'd placed name placards on each desk. Oak wasn't the only one who wondered how the new girl's name was pronounced. Everyone laughed when the teacher called out "Lazoolee," but that had been Oak's guess, too.

"It's *Laz*-you-lye. As in lapis lazuli." She'd explained — in the most glorious of voices — that when her father first saw the color of her eyes, he'd thought of the semiprecious stones found in Egypt.

Oak thought the name was almost as beautiful as the girl. Those striking blue eyes radiated serenity, while a pert nose, ivory complexion, high cheekbones, and full lips completed the charming picture. She was beautiful, but it was her ready smile that won hearts. Everyone adored her.

"Lazy, watch it. Stoneface is coming." This from Fluff, a large, sleek-haired girl whose colorless eyes reminded Oak of a frosty winter day.

Eulila quickly doffed the cloche and moved toward the hat display. Fluff linked arms with Lazuli and guided her away from the mirror. The next instant, Lazuli was entangled in a rack of dresses. She struggled to detach herself.

"Oh, be careful, Lazy! Here, let me help." Fluff looked like she was helping her friend, but Oak saw her grab more dresses and fling them to the floor — all while pretending to pull Lazuli out of the tangle.

"Say!" Oak started toward them, then stopped.

"What is going on here?" The manager's voice was commanding.

"Nothing, Mrs. Stone. Lazuli had an accident and I was helping her. We're trying to straighten up this terrible mess."

"Do it quickly, then. What will the customers think if they see this?" Mrs. Stone smoothed her brow, nervously watching the two young ladies replace the dresses on wooden hangers and hang them up neatly. When everything was in order again, they stood aside for Mrs. Stone's inspection. The older woman nodded curtly and then turned on her heel.

"That woman's mouth is pursed so tightly, it's hard to tell which end is up some days."

"Fluff!"

"You know it's true, Lazy. Come on, I could use a break . . ." Their voices faded as they walked toward the far staircase.

"Son, have you found a suit?"

Oak, who had been watching Lazuli and Fluff, switched his attention to his mother. "Mother, what do you think of Fluff?"

Eulila pulled a loose thread on Oak's shoulder. Her eyes didn't meet her son's. "Why do you ask, dear?"

"It's just — oh, never mind. Mother, I like this suit, but I'm afraid it costs too much."

Eulila looked at the tag. "Go ahead, Oak. Buy it. I've got some store credit plus a discount." She turned her son one way, then the other. "You look good. Tell Harry I'll bring the suit home with me."

"You're a peach, Mother."

"You don't say?"

Oak held his breath as he dropped off a folded newspaper at the new hair salon. JazzBaby Bobs had opened recently on Main Street and sported a steady flow of flappers. It was beyond him what went on inside, but whatever it was, it rankled the nostrils.

A sign on the window advertised:

Bobbed Hair
*Gives a good chance to make
your scalp healthy and your
hair more beautiful and life-like.*

At least once a week use
MULSIFIED COCOANUT
OIL SHAMPOO
The results are pleasing.
50¢ and $1.00 sizes

For some time, there had been a fiery controversy over bobbed hair in Grand Junction. It was the tip of the iceberg in a tug-of-war between prim Victorian traditions and "Modern" thinking. This battle had split many families, and even the town.

The Daily Sentinel had taken advantage of the controversy by presenting an unbiased column called "Bobbed Heads." It was highly successful as dozens of lively letters arrived daily, full of accusations, stories of woe, and tales of satisfaction and conviction. There was even poetry.

The prevailing philosophy of those who bobbed their hair was much more than an adolescent rebellion against the status quo. It was breaking the obsolete molds that had been ruling society — unsuccessfully in their minds — and replacing them with new, meaningful ones.

When his bag was empty, Oak gratefully sank into a wrought iron chair at Mesa Drug. A new waitress shambled over. She looked about as old as Oak's younger sister, Grace, but there was a fine network of lines around her snappy eyes.

"Hey, toots, whatchawant?" Her voice was as coarse as seawater. She leaned close, bestowing him with a warm smile. A *very* warm smile.

Oak did a double take. "Strawberry malted. Please."

"Sprinkles?"

Oak got a whiff of her 10¢ glamour girl perfume, and he pulled on his collar. "Er, why not?"

"Right-e-o. My name's Pansy."

The waitress turned away and winked over her shoulder at Oak. He wasn't sure what to do with that wink. It was his first one. His face hot, he looked around.

A long counter flanked the west side of the store, each end curving into the wall, hemming in the soda jerk and his tasty accoutrements. Behind the counter an ornate mirror, supported by an equally ornate cherry wood cabinet, spanned the enclosure. Underneath the smooth, polished countertop, metal stools waited for patrons. Menus and a Coca Cola sign were displayed prominently.

Several glass and wood cases lined the opposite wall, holding cigars and an array of magazines. At the back of the store, the pharmacy had several people waiting in line.

Hank Philips, the soda jerk, expertly crafted ice cream, fruit, malt, soda water, whipped cream, and sprinkles into a work of art. His pristine image was reflected in the mirror: a white uniform with creases down each sleeve and a boat-shaped hat square on his shiny parted hair.

There were five wrought iron tables on the waxed linoleum floor, and Oak sat at one of them. Near the front window, he saw Evan's wife, Margaret, and Lillian Gesberg sitting with their heads together, talking animatedly. Margaret's wheat-hued hair was woven into a braid that hung down the back of her blue sailor dress.

In the past, when a lady's "delicate condition" began to show, she went into self-imposed exile until the baby was born. Nowadays, the modern woman with child enjoyed a new freedom, and it was obvious Margaret Treece was taking advantage of that. She rested one hand on her protruding belly, and with the other she dipped her spoon into a scoop of pink ice cream.

Lillian was a dark contrast to Margaret. A white cloche hat was pulled down on her mahogany bob and the frilled hem of her lavender dress nearly touched the floor as she sat. She smiled often, revealing a gap between her two front teeth. Oak assumed Lillian, who worked at the Fair with his mother, was on break.

Pansy sidled up to the ladies and asked if there was anything else they needed. Margaret looked at her friend, who shook her head. She lifted her elfish face to the waitress and softly said, "You are finished with us." The waitress seemed taken aback.

"She means we are finished," explained Lillian. "Thank you."

"Oh. Well, ladies, I hope you both enjoyed your visit at Mesa Drug. 'Quality of Merchandise with a High Standard of Service' is our motto. Please come again." She slapped a ticket on the table.

Margaret brushed a wisp of hair behind her ear and nodded. Lillian stood up and kissed the other girl's cheek. "Mags, this was the cat's meow. Thanks for meeting me. I LOVE the baby bonnet you knitted. Now I want you to let me know if there's anything I can do for you. Okey-dokey?"

The two got up and separated at the door. Oak was amazed at their friendship. They were so different from each other: Lillian, tall, confident, and athletic; Margaret — a pale waif who would never learn a language, tally her grocery bill, or read a book.

If it wasn't for Evan, Margaret would have been sent to the State Home for Mental Defectives, on the edge of the town, to live out her days. Fortunately, Evan had fallen in love and married the girl. It looked as though the union had benefited both. Evan, who had been a bit wild in his youth, had settled down, and Margaret had blossomed with Evan's love. She was able to do simple but necessary things, such as take care of herself and the house, and her devotion to her husband was obvious.

When the waitress returned with Oak's malted perched on a small plate, she pointed out the extra sprinkles. "Hank said that was for helpin' his little sister cross the street the other day."

Oak raised his spoon to the soda jerk. "Anyone would have done it, but thanks."

Pansy looked at him. "Applesauce! Not everyone takes the time to help someone in need, you know." She turned to go.

"Uh, Pansy, are you new in town?"

She turned around, surprise on her face. "Gee whiz, thanks for askin'. Came in on the train a couple of nights ago. Talk about helpin' in time of need; some young fella in a brand new car pointed me in the direction of a gal named Nell Page. She took me right in off the street. Nice lady. But," here the woman bent close to Oak's ear, "I think there might be some hanky-panky goin' on. She has a *lot* of male visitors."

"That's because — "

"What?"

"Never mind." How could he tell her she was staying in the most notorious section of town? Oak looked critically at Pansy. There'd be hell to pay when she did find out.

Chapter Two

T hat night, Main Street was lit up with music, chatter, and glittering dresses. Storm clouds had dissipated after the rain, and the evening sky was clear and crisp.

Oak had parked the old Ford Model T a block away on Colorado Avenue and joined the throng of students in climbing the worn, wooden stairs to Margery Hall. His excitement grew as he moved upward.

Momentarily, he thought of his mother. He hoped she wasn't in too much trouble on his account. His father had been working in the garden when she'd pushed Oak out the front door, saying all was well. He doubted it, but she was a peach for intervening.

Inside the double doors, Oak took in the scene. Immense tables were set for about two hundred guests and small favors and balloons decorated each plate. Class colors were in abundance, and at the ends of the room, two tall, beautifully gilded replicas of class pins represented the juniors and seniors.

Oak found a seat near a corner to give him the best view of the room. He considered it necessary, as a reporter, to be a people watcher. The tables gradually filled up, and the meal was served. Oak was disappointed to not see Lazuli among the guests. Perhaps she was ill. *Damn!*

According to the program he received at the door, the LaCourt Hotel's own kitchen had catered the elegant dinner. It took nearly an hour for the four courses to be presented: Stuffed Tomatoes in Aspic Jelly and Frozen Cheese to start; followed by choice of Broiled Beefsteak with Yorkshire Pudding or Chicken Quenelles; Cream Asparagus; and to drink, Blackberry Ice Blocks with Lemonade. For dessert there was Baked Alaska.

After the dinner, the faculty and junior class stood up and toasted the graduates, taking turns with a megaphone. Tender memories were resurrected by faculty and student body; some were funny and some brought forth bittersweet tears. After that, little gifts were handed out. Before things got too maudlin, the tables were put away to make room for the dance floor.

Evan and Margaret Treece stood behind the linen-draped refreshment table, administering punch to students. Oak waded through the crowd until he reached the couple. Evan's wiry hair was plastered down with pomade. Although he wore a suit to work every day, he looked uncomfortable without his overalls and apron. He kept shoving his hands in his pockets.

"Are you guarding the punch?" Oak knew someone would try to spike it, even though booze was illegal.

"Don't want kids embalmed on my watch."

"Party pooper," Oak kidded.

Evan grinned.

Prohibition kept Bert Watson and his two deputies busy chasing stills down and crashing drinking parties in private homes. Yet Grand Junction's speakeasies flourished under their noses, and nearly every young man had a flask of moonshine in his back pocket. Everyone, including the authorities, knew the "Grand Experiment" had failed, but it was still the law of the land.

"You will dance, Oak." Margaret was wearing a beribboned yellow shift that strained against her abdomen.

Oak concentrated on the pale freckles that dotted her nose. He embraced modern thinking but still struggled with the unrestricted revelation of the female body. "I'm getting my bearings. And a glass of punch, if you don't mind." Oak smiled at Margaret.

"Yes."

She dipped into the lime green liquid and shyly offered Oak a dripping cup. He took a napkin and dabbed the bottom before heading to the bank of windows in the back — the usual place for wallflowers. He passed Dugger Snyder, who snickered when he saw Oak. Leaning toward Hal's ear, he whispered something, and they both laughed heartily. Oak tried to ignore it but felt a slow heat suffuse his neck.

Settling into his regular space, Oak looked curiously at the girl standing next to him. The unpunched dance card she held tightly in her hand was as conspicuous as her whitened face, coiffed hair, and bright red and blue peacocks strutting across her silk kimono. He almost suggested she might as well go to the Mahjong table in the corner because she certainly wasn't going to dance, but didn't have the heart. Mahjong apparel may be the latest craze for wives of rich businessmen, but certainly not for high school seniors. *Her mother probably suggested that getup.*

Come to think of it, *his* mother had given her blessing on the suit he was wearing. Resigned, Oak glanced sideways and sighed. *Birds of a feather . . .*

Nearby, a group of students surrounded Dalton Trumbo and his girlfriend, Sylvia Longshore. She was a year younger than Dalton and an excellent dancer. Her father owned an ice cream factory. Dalton had his arm around the girl, basking in his peers' admiration.

"You must know I was one of the students that voted for you to receive the Templeman cup, Dalton."

"All-around leadership — well done, my boy!"

Several seniors clapped Dalton on the shoulder. His mouth formed a confident smile, while his eyes slid past the admiring crowd to Oak. He nodded and raised his punch glass to him.

It took a split second for Oak to realize the man he admired the most was actually saluting him! He quickly returned the favor, spilling some liquid on his sleeve. Swearing under his breath, he pulled a handkerchief from his breast pocket and patted the stain. When he looked up again, Dalton's attention had returned to those gathered around him. Pleasantly stunned, Oak wandered back to the punchbowl.

He had lived in Grand Junction all his life, yet he had no close friends. Although he recognized every person in the room and could relate a litany of known and little known facts about each one, there wasn't a soul he could comfortably clap on the shoulder and say, "Well done, my boy!"

Oak had come to terms with his role in life by the time he'd left elementary school. The ability to melt into the woodwork was a mixed blessing. It enabled him to watch life unnoticed, an advantage to a reporter, but people's true colors were often revealed when they thought no one was watching. Oak had seen plenty that humbled, as well as shocked, him. Strangely, while the world seemed to care less about Oak, he wanted to make that same world a better place.

"Another?" Evan refilled Oak's empty cup. "I haven't seen you once on the dance floor. There's plenty of 'shegas,' as you call the girls. What's the problem?"

Oak shook his head, chuckling. "*Shebas*, Evan. Haven't found any *shebas* I want to embarrass myself with."

"How about her?"

Oak followed Evan's gaze to the entrance. Lazuli shimmered in a rose-accented, knee-length gown. A matching hair band decorated her blonde hair, which glowed under the globed tungsten lights. A silver mesh purse dangled from her posed hand and a long strand of pearls swished unimpeded across her flat chest.

There was a momentary lull as she made her entrance. Every eye in the room, besides Oak's, had swiveled to the doorway. The next moment, Lazuli fell unceremoniously on her face.

"Lazy, are you all right?" Fluff, looking like a purple powder puff, was leaning over the prostrate girl. Oak reached Lazuli before the rest of the men in the room did.

"My goodness!" Fluff said, when Oak pushed her aside.

"Your goodness has nothing to do with this," Oak said, giving Fluff a warning look. "I saw what you did."

"I was just trying to help."

Oak turned his back on the pouting girl and offered his hand to Lazuli. She looked up, a bit dazed, and took Oak's hand. Her poise had slid back in place by the time she stood to her feet.

Lazuli smiled at the concerned males pressing in around her. "Put those flasks away, boys, before you get into trouble. Besides, I'd like something," here she looked at Oak, "less potent."

"Can I get you something? A punch?" Oak hadn't realized the girl was as tall as he.

"A steady hand, if you please," her eyes were amused. "Then a drink. Punch."

With Herculean effort, Oak calmed his shaking, but by then his stomach began to make strange wheezing sounds. Oak surreptitiously slugged the offending organ. He guided Lazuli to the punchbowl, while Fluff followed, mewing protestations.

After Oak handed Lazuli her drink, Fluff held out a pudgy hand. "You may get me a cup, too — er, what *is* your name?"

"Oak." He indicated to Evan to give Fluff a punch. "Miller. That is to say, Oak Miller. All together."

Lazuli grinned. "Well, Oak Miller, all together, you are a gentleman." She downed her cup in one gulp, then gazed around.

"I suppose I'd better schmooze before the night slips further away." She laid her empty cup on the table. "Thank you, Oak."

"L-Lazuli? May I buy a dance? Later, that is. Only if you want to." Warm sweat drizzled from his armpits. Oak clenched his arms to his side.

"Are you all right?"

"Yup."

"That's debatable, I'm sure." Dugger Snyder was at Lazuli's elbow. "She won't have time for the likes of you, Miller. She's saved her dance card for the best-looking fella in the room. Me." Dugger wedged between Lazuli and Oak, stepping on Oak's toe in the process. Oak winced and moved back.

"Dugger, you goat," Lazuli gently pushed Dugger out of the way. His jaw tightened, Oak noticed with satisfaction. "Don't be rude. Of course, I'll save a dance for you, Oak."

"Not likely, chum." Fluff smirked as she followed the couple to the dance floor. Along the way, she jerked a tall, skinny boy out of the crowd and began swinging him around.

Sighing, Oak had to admit Lazuli and Dugger danced well together. The perfect sheik and sheba.

Near ten o clock, Oak had yet to dance with Lazuli. He wandered to the men's restroom. There was a line as the men's room accommodated only one person at a time. Oak assumed the ladies' room was more resplendent as small groups eddied in and out of the windowed door. While he waited, Lazuli flew by with a look of the hunted.

"L-lazuli? Hi, remember me? Oak?"

"Of course I remember my *hero*." Lazuli stopped and placed a graceful hand on Oak's arm.

His need for the bathroom increased dramatically. Moving from one foot to the other he stammered, "May I have the pleasure of a dance?"

"Here?" Lazuli's silky voice followed her eyes as she glanced up and down the hallway.

"Bless me, no." Oak took a deep breath.

"You are such a funny little darb." Lazuli pulled out a card from her purse and peered at it. "All of them seem to be paid for, Oak." She lifted his crestfallen face with a gentle finger. "Except the last one. I saved that one *especially* for you. Free gratis."

"It would be my — "

"Lazy, where are you?"

Irritation rippled across Lazuli's features. "Don't forget, Oak, last dance." Then she was gone.

Like I could forget!

A few moments later, Fluff rushed around the corner, giving him an accusatory glare. Oak was beginning to appreciate the fact that he wasn't popular. Poor Lazuli seemed to be everyone's prey. He watched Fluff elbow her way into the ladies' restroom.

"*There* you are — " The closing door bit off Fluff's words.

When Oak came out of the men's room, Dalton Trumbo was leaning against the far wall, near a standing brass ashtray. He had a cigarette stuck in the side of his mouth.

"That girl is something else."

Oak looked back to see if Dalton was talking to someone behind him. They were alone. "Beg pardon?"

"Fluff." He raised his chin toward the bathroom. "Ridiculous name, but it fits her. Tell me, do you think the person lives up to the name, or does the name dictate who the person will be?" A puff of smoke sped lazily toward the vaulted ceiling. "Take yours, for instance. I read that an oak tree grows stronger when the wind is contrary."

Dalton pulled a slim cigarette case out of his jacket pocket, flipped it open, and offered one to Oak. Unconsciously, he took it.

"You know my name?"

"I've known it for a while. Rarely do these eyes," Dalton tapped his temple, "miss anything. You were the only person who didn't make fun of me, Oak. I've been watching you ever since."

"But, you've ig — "

"One usually smokes those things."

Oak looked down at his hands. He'd shredded the cigarette. Shoving the remnants into his pockets, he looked down at his feet.

"So, what about it?"

"Huh?"

"Your name."

"Oh. Mother named me Oak because the doctor dropped me on my head at birth and I lived. She said my head had to be as hard as oak."

"You don't say? I haven't a clue why I was named Dalton. How do you live up to a name that has no meaning?"

"You've done well not knowing, I'd say." Oak now understood how Dalton, the reporter, got to the heart of a matter. He made people comfortable.

Dalton chuckled. "Perhaps that was the key."

"What are you doing now that you graduated? Heard you were quitting the *Sentinel.*"

"Got a better paying job at Currie Canning. After summer, I'll be hauling my one suitcase to Boulder for college. Walter Walker," the publisher's name rolled familiarly off Dalton's tongue, "keeps encouraging me to go into politics, but I don't think I could stand the stink."

"Not everyone in public office is crooked."

"I have my hopes with our president, 'Silent Cal,' but it's hard to trust. Washington is in the midst of that Teapot Dome scandal." Oak had to agree. "What I really want to do is write the 'Great American Novel.' Maybe win a Pulitzer Prize."

"If anyone can do it, you can, Dalton."

"I appreciate the confidence. Time will tell if it's misplaced or not. What about you?"

"Father wants me at the shop, but I — "

The door to the ladies' room opened and Fluff and Lazuli came out, arm in arm. They seemed on friendly terms.

"See you soon, doll?" Before disappearing around the corner, Lazuli smiled at Oak over her shoulder. Fluff scowled over hers.

"Yes, soon." Oak's voice petered out.

Dalton looked amused. "She seems interested."

"Hardly. I'm surprised she's looked twice at me. Once was more than I ever expected."

"You don't give yourself enough credit."

"On the contrary, I know exactly how much credit to give myself."

"Do you?" Dalton cocked an eyebrow at Oak before snuffing his cigarette out in the ashtray.

"Dalton, may I ask you a question?"

"Fire away."

"Who's taking your beat?"

The other man looked steadily at Oak. "Would you like to give it a try?"

Oak couldn't believe his luck! The girl of his dreams was saving a dance for him and the fellow he most wanted to be like was offering him a big break. The two men made plans to meet at Mesa Drug the next day, after Oak had delivered his papers. They both walked back into the dance hall. Oak felt taller.

The Charleston was playing; the room in full throttle, with arms and legs at frantic angles. It reminded Oak of a horde of grasshoppers foraging.

Off in the corner, the Treeces were cleaning up the refreshment table. Things seemed to be winding down. With his new confidence, Oak searched for Lazuli. She broke into a wide smile when she saw him, stepping out of the melee to greet him.

"Ready for our dance?"

"Yup."

"Not so fast!" Dugger's hostile face appeared. "This one ain't over, yet. Come on, Laz," He reached for the girl's hand.

She pulled it away. "I believe I'll rest this one out, Duggie."

"Why do you want to waste time with this nobody? Come on, I said."

He grasped her, pulling. Lazuli cried out. Before he knew it, Oak had gotten between the two and stuck a fist to Dugger's nose. The music stopped and the room became still. Oak sensed everyone watching.

Yowzah! What have I gotten myself into?

"Humph. Think you can take me on?"

"What I think is you're a big bully."

"You gonna let him talk to you like that?" Fluff had appeared behind Dugger, along with Hal and Chas.

"That's enough, Fluff." Lazuli rubbed her wrist. "As a matter of fact, I think I hear the last dance starting," she said, nodding to the leader of the band. "Follow me," Lazuli said, close to Oak's ear.

Mr. Brown took his cue and started "On The Blue Lagoon." Oak and Dugger exchanged menacing sneers, before Oak took Lazuli in his arms on the dance floor. Couples tentatively joined them.

"You're trembling," Lazuli said.

Oak refrained from telling her his legs were made of Jell-O. "Isn't this how one waltzes?"

"Silly boy. Relax."

Every full swing around the room, he caught sight of the malevolent group around Dugger.

"You're trembling again, Oak. Whatever's the matter?"

"There's a chill in here." Oak chastised himself. *The dance of a lifetime and your attention is on that moron!* He dedicated the rest of the dance to Lazuli. Oak's feet felt twice their size, but Lazuli guided him around the polished wood floor flawlessly, while seeming to follow her partner. Oak soon caught on, and the roles reversed. They fit well together and flowed around the dance floor as one. Lazuli chattered the whole time; Oak memorized every tiny detail of her face. When the music faded, Oak dragged his eyes away from his partner and, strangely, the color seemed to drain from his vision. It was like watching a movie at the Majestic.

"Lazuli," Oak stammered, "you are so beautiful, even the rainbow loses its bloom beside you."

"Why, Oak — " Lazuli looked embarrassed.

Even the rainbow loses its bloom? Buffoon! Oak thought he was going to be sick.

The purple Fluff saved the moment. "I want to go home." She'd marched up to them, folding her arms.

You and me both, toots. Yowzah! Did I say that out loud?

Fluff glowered at Oak. "You'll take us."

Maybe not. "Us?"

"That's a great idea! We came together, Oak." Lazuli's brow furrowed. "If you don't mind?"

"It would be my pleasure."

"Good. We'll meet you downstairs. Let's get our wraps, Fluff."

As soon as the Ford squeaked to a stop in front of the Margery Building, Lazuli and Fluff got in. "Take Lazy home first. I live up on Orchard Mesa and she needs to get home by eleven thirty."

Pulling his pocket watch out, he noted that left ten minutes. His own curfew, one of the many rules his father was a stickler for, was midnight. He'd barely make it to Orchard Mesa and back in time. Oak was disappointed. He'd hoped to share his remaining minutes with Lazuli, perhaps find the courage to ask her for a date — while his confidence was hovering above nil.

Just a few blocks away, on Seventh Street, Oak was directed to park. He stared at the lighted house — a mansion, really — with its manicured lawn and trimmed bushes. His expectations sunk. There was no way this beautiful, rich, popular girl would want to spend an evening with him. *Silly boy.* Oak stumbled out of the Ford and opened Lazuli's door.

Fluff stared balefully at them. "Hurry up, will you?"

Oak resisted the urge to stick out his tongue at her. He slowly walked Lazuli to her front door, hating the moment he'd have to say good night.

"*Sherlock, Jr.* is showing at the Majestic next Friday. I love Buster Keaton."

Oak blinked. "Are — are you asking me on a date?"

"Well, if I waited for you to ask, hell would freeze over." She leaned over and kissed Oak's cheek.

"Pick you up at seven!" Oak managed to utter. He trotted back to the auto, fearing Lazuli would change her mind before she got inside. And he needed to sit down.

"Now, wasn't that sweet?" Fluff's eyes glittered in the dark.

Turn here, at Four Corners. There's my house. Fluff had been quiet as the Ford jostled over the railroad tracks, then up

the Fifth Street Bridge spanning the Colorado River, to
Orchard Mesa.

The clay roads had dried fast following the afternoon
downpour, and Oak was thankful. He hated putting tire chains
on, especially in the mud.

Oak was familiar with the area. Even back when the
Colorado River had been called the Grand, his mother had
brought him and Grace here for Sunday teas or parties. They'd
ride their bicycles most times, but sometimes Mother would
splurge, and they'd take the Ford. Several of the Fair employees,
including John Gesberg, lived up here, though his house was one
of the farthest away.

Oak pulled up in front of a two-story farmhouse, fronted
by a tiny fenced yard. The waxing moon barely illuminated the
surrounding tilled fields, which stretched outward in ghostly
waves. Sitting in the gravel driveway, the shiny curves of a
Model T coupe were outlined. "Nice jalopy, Fluff! It looks just
like D — "

"Gotta go."

Oak didn't think girls her size could move so fast. The front
door closed with a slam. Checking his pocket watch, he saw he
had just enough time to get home. Putting the Ford in reverse, he
turned to check behind him. Out of the darkness, a fist slammed
into his face. Oak saw stars.

"So, you wanna steal my girl, do ya?" Oak saw spittle on
Dugger s lip right before another wallop of pain wiped out con-
sciousness.

"Hey, you ragamuffins! Cut that out!"

Oak thought he must be in heaven, the light was so brilliant.
Then he heard an auto start; its engine muffling the farther away

it sped. Oak sighed. Not heaven. The Bible never mentions automobiles in that glorious place. A shame.

Oak's situation slowly seeped in. He lay on the ground, someone's headlights bathing him in light. Road ruts dug into his back. *Damn.* His mother would be angry about his new suit being dirty. He was working out a plausible excuse, when he felt someone lifting him.

"Are you all right?" Sturdy hands held Oak aloft.

"I'm truly sorry, Mother." At least that's what he tried to say. Oak stuck out his tongue and felt his bottom lip. Swollen. *How'd that happen?*

"Son, I ain't your 'buther.' You sure you're all right?"

Light haloed around Oak's rescuer, but Oak recognized Harold Gesberg, one of John's sons. "Hey, Mr. Gesberg. What am I doing here?" He felt drunk, but didn't remember imbibing. *Whatever I drank, it packed a punch!*

"Daddy, is the big boy hurt?" Out of the dark interior of Gesberg's auto came a little girl's voice.

"Nothing a porterhouse steak can't take care of, Bernice. You go on back to sleep," the man called, without turning around. "Good thing Carl and Charlotte's serenade party ran late. No telling how long you'da lain in a puddle like that." He half-dragged Oak to his vehicle and gently situated him in the front seat. "Gather your wits, then get on home, Oak. And choose your friends more wisely."

The crisp night air cleared Oak's head. He tasted blood, and the memories flooded back. His glance wobbled to Fluff's house and he observed an upstairs curtain slip into place. "In light of the situation, Mr. Gesberg, I guess you're a better friend than most. Thanks."

Harold grinned. "Well, I'm not sure I like being called 'Bister' Gesberg, but I take your meaning. You might find 'Harold' easier to say." He touched his brow as he got behind his steering wheel. "You're a good man, Oak."

Oak nodded, though pain shot in all directions. Funny, he felt more like a fool.

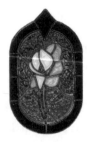

Chapter Three

"What happened to you, son?"

Oak was reading the funny section of the *Denver Post*, trying not to laugh at the new comic strip, "Mutt and Jeff."

"Oak is in trouble, his lip's a big fat bubble, his black eye's seeing double . . ." Grace sang softly behind the front pages of the paper.

He reached over and tapped her paper. She stopped singing but continued humming behind it. Oak sighed. Why is it the only time he was noticed was when he didn't want to be?

Sunlight shone through the yellow curtains of the small kitchen, glowing against the daisy wallpaper. This was the brightest area in the six-room bungalow. Robert ruled the rest of the roost, with its long-faced demeanor, but this room belonged to his wife. And Eulila Miller's kitchen *smiled*.

She tied an apron behind her back and opened the icebox by the back door. "Grace, put the newspaper down and get the milk bottles, please."

Grace tossed the paper onto the table and opened the back door. Resting on the stoop were two fresh bottles of frosty milk delivered by Rose Glen Dairy. She picked them up and deposited them on the counter next to her mother.

"It's cold this morning. Summer is *never* going to come!" Grace rubbed her hands together and again disappeared behind the morning news.

"Nonsense. It's just late this year. Oak, I asked you a question, young man."

Setting a recipe book against the toaster, Eulila checked off the ingredients she needed for breakfast. She was trying something called waffles, cooked on a waffle iron, the newest invention to find a home in her kitchen. It paid to work at the Fair, where store stock was deeply discounted for employees. She took the edge of her apron and polished a non-existent spot on the large, shiny, mushroom-shaped appliance next to her glass bowl.

"Got smacked by an enthusiastic dancer." He lowered the funnies and mumbled, "Until then, it had been a wonderful evening." Lazuli came to mind, and Oak's swollen lip curved. A sliver of pain ended any further sentiment.

Grace giggled. "You sound funny, Oak!"

Eulila whisked the batter briskly, then she poured some of it onto the iron. The room quickly filled with the aroma of vanilla. Oak's stomach responded noisily.

"It says here 721 people in Chicago died of automobile wrecks last year, 227 of them children. Over 7,000 were injured!" Grace rustled the paper down, a look of incredulity on her face. "Why haven't people learned to be careful? The slaughter of the innocents, these unfortunate pedestrians, goes on ruthlessly by careless drivers. And the foolish pedestrians! Why haven't they learned to stay out of the way of the modern juggernaut?" Eulila and Oak stared at Grace. "Well, it's true!"

"*How* old are you, sis?" Oak poured honey over his waffle and cut into it. "Mmm, this dish is delish!" Wincing, he touched his lip. *Until the swelling goes down, I'll have to choose my words carefully.*

Grace's paper wall went up again. "You know I'm twelve-years-old, Oak."

"Twelve going on a hundred. Sometimes I think you were born old."

"Mother! Oak's picking on me!" Grace glared at her brother over the top of the paper.

"*That's* more like it." Oak winked at his sister and stood up. He started to kiss his mother's cheek, but stopped short. He patted her shoulder, instead. "I'll be working in the yard until deliveries." He let the back door slam shut.

Eulila watched her son drag a wheelbarrow from the shed. He piled on a rake and shovel and disappeared around the corner. "I shudder to think about what *really* happened to that boy." She shook her head and attended to the next waffle. "Grace, here's your breakfast. Oh hello, Robert. How long have you been standing there? I'll have a waffle for you in a moment."

"What's a waffle?"

"It's something that looks *very* peculiar," tolled Grace's grave voice.

"If your mother cooked it, I'm sure it's acceptable." Robert sat down next to Grace and gently pried the newspaper from her hands. She resisted for a second, then gave in.

"Don't read the article about automobile accidents. It will upset your tummy." Grace fluttered her eyelashes at her father, then picked up her fork and dug into her waffle.

Robert looked suspiciously at his daughter, who had begun humming a funeral dirge. He shook the paper straight. "Lila, that boy came home near two o'clock in the morning. Even after the city curfew. He could have been arrested! He needs to be knocked down to size, I tell you."

"Robert, have some compassion. How often does one graduate from high school? That 'boy' has grown up, so you better start letting him make some decisions on his own." Eulila kissed her husband's brow before placing a plate in front of him. "You've got to start trusting him, sometime."

Robert picked up his fork. "I'll start trusting him when he starts acting responsibly. Disobedience deserves punishment. He didn't even stay and help me weed last night."

"He's working outside now, dear. Can't you forgive him this one time?"

"I'm loathe to do that."

"But Robert — "

"But me no buts, Lila. The boy has got to learn his lesson. I'll talk to him tonight."

Eulila leaned against the counter and scrutinized her husband. She remembered a time when those almond eyes were toasted with affection and that gentle mouth smiled easily. How she missed the pre-war Robert. Now an invisible gate guarded those beloved features, a NO TRESPASSING sign tacked securely on. Robert was difficult, impossible at times. Still, she couldn't imagine life without him.

"Come on, Worrywart. I'll drop you off at the Carnegie Library." She removed her apron and shuffled Grace to the back door. "I need to take the Ford, dear. Piggly Wiggly has green beans on sale, and I want to beat the rush."

"You realize ethyl has gone up? Don't be wasting my hard-earned money, Lila."

Eulila didn't bother to answer. "I'll clean up after I get back from shopping. I don't have to be at the Fair until noon. Pick you up tonight?"

"Humph."

"Lillian, that dress does wonders for you. You simply glow, my dear." Eulila closed the little door to her locker, number thirty-two, sticking the key in a tiny pocket on her waistband.

Eulila, Lillian Gesberg, Wilma Anderegg, and her younger sister, Yum, were in the ladies dressing room, a comfortable place lined with lockers on one side and stuffed chairs beside end tables along the other. A long, low bench divided the business side from the area of relaxation. The men had their own dressing room across the hallway.

"I see you've chosen the emerald one-piece slip-on, with front and back plaits, oval neckline, and short kimono sleeves. A lovely choice, madam," Wilma said in her best sales clerk voice.

The women giggled around Lillian, admiring her newest dress. The twenty-year-old was the "fashion plate" of the Fair Store. She'd been the first to purchase a flapper dress from Women's Ready-to-Wear when the Fair's New York buyer began shipping them the year before.

Eulila looked at her own dress, which she'd made from a Butterick pattern purchased at the Fair. It was simple, yet similar to the styles most of her patrons wore. And a lot less expensive.

"The lines are so straight! You're really hep, Lil! It's perfect for your slender figure," chimed in Yum.

Saturdays, Yum stocked shelves at the Fair. She would start high school in the fall, yet she still had a bit of the girl about her. Eulila watched as Yum fawned over Lillian, obviously her hero.

Lillian kissed the girl's cheek. "That's well and good for now, my friends, but my figure won't be boyish for very long." She looked mysterious.

"Do tell, Lil!"

"No, *you* tell *me* — does this hat go with the dress?" Lillian placed a small hat on her head, its leather-stitched brim folded up with a spray of straw jutting at an angle.

This elicited oohs and ahs from the group.

The door to the dressing room opened and Mrs. Stone's stern face made an appearance. It dampened the gaiety immediately. "The floor is waiting, ladies."

"Yes, ma'am," the women said in unison.

The door closed firmly.

"That old fossil!" Yum mimicked Mrs. Stone's matriarchal drawl. "*The floor is waiting!*"

Everyone but Eulila laughed. "Just because a woman is old doesn't mean she shouldn't be treated with respect."

"But she *thinks* old, too. She believes a girl's hair is her glory!" Yum protested.

"And why shouldn't it be?" Eulila pulled out the pins that held her sausage curls in place. They cascaded down her back.

"Your hair is lovely, Eulila," said Wilma, "but so is bobbed hair. And, unlike long hair, you can wash and comb it *every day.* Most times, long hair looks matted and dusty — not yours, of course — because it's only washed once or twice a month. Unsightly! Dangerous, too.

"Why, I read about a lady who died because a black widow had taken up residence in her bun. It bit her and her husband found her dead in bed next morning, with her eyes swollen shut."

"Yowzah!" Yum drew back.

"You mustn't believe everything you read in the newspapers," Eulila said, putting a maternal arm across Yum's shoulders.

"Why ever not? They only tell the truth," Wilma said. She raised a stubborn chin. "Besides, bobbed hair means you're "modern." Mrs. Stone and her ilk would have us still attending Victorian teas and handkerchief parties. They'd want us to mind our husbands and settle for teaching or being a nanny if we want a career. We have rights, too, and — " Wilma's face started to crumple, "no one should dictate how we women should live our lives!"

"You obviously feel strongly about this."

Wilma burst into tears and buried her face in Eulila's shoulder.

"My land, child. There's no need to get so emotional. If it makes you feel better, I'll think about bobbing my hair."

"It's not only that," Wilma cried thickly. "Leonard, he — oh, I shouldn't be talking. It's only, things haven't been that peaceful at our house lately. I don't know if he's reacting to his mother's illness or he's dissatisfied with me. I'm afraid our Betty is privy to shouting matches, and that's not good for a young'un. I'm not sure what to do."

"How is Rachel doing?"

Wilma sniffed. "You know she was sent off to the cancer sanitarium in Missouri last February? I know doctors have made great strides in treating that dread disease, but I'm afraid she's not long for this world. Her letters are full of such sad things."

Wilma pulled out a letter from her pocket and read:

> *"I am so weak I can't walk. I never thought I could get so weak so soon, but I have a hard case, with a spot as big as a dinner plate. At least they are not taking both my breasts, like my roommate."*

"Leonard wants me to stay home, our marriage is falling apart, Rachel is suffering terribly, and there's nothing I can do!" Wilma sobbed into her hands. "Why do things have to change so much?"

"I'm sorry, Wilma," Yum patted her sister's shoulder.

"Me, too." Lillian knelt in front of the distraught woman. "I'm sure your mother-in-law is being treated with the best of modern medicine. We can only pray for her and hope she gets better.

"Now, regarding your husband; it will pass, dear. These things generally do. Art gets into a snit every once in a while," Lillian's eyes softened at the mention of her husband, "but he always comes 'round."

Lillian's optimism wasn't shared by Eulila, who knew that many circumstances in life, including having cancer, didn't pass. "We'll all pray for your family," she said. Everyone nodded.

Wilma withdrew a snowy handkerchief from her pocket and blew her nose. "Thanks, girls. Sorry for the waterworks."

"I know something that will cheer everyone up," Lillian beamed. "If I share a secret, you won't tell Art I told you, will you?" Everyone eagerly shook their heads.

"I'm you-know-what!" She flattened her dress across her abdomen, and a slight bulge emerged. The room filled with squeals. "Four months along. It's a miracle at that, given how poor Ana is the only Gesberg wife who has conceived, bless little Bernice.

"Poor Art, losing Ruth to scarlet fever. I've tried to be the best wife, but it seems Ruth's ghost is always between us. A child would stop his sadness, I just know it!"

"It will, Lil."

"Art is so excited. We both think it's a girl."

"How sweet! But what makes you think the baby is a girl?" asked Wilma.

"It's silly, but I had a dream," Lillian lowered her voice to a whisper. "The baby was about six months old, and had dark hair, sparkling blue eyes, and the most adorable dimples when she smiled. The dream was so real, when I woke up I went in search of her." Lillian sneezed several times in a row. "Excuse me. I must be allergic to something." She accepted the handkerchief Yum offered. "Anyway, I can't wait to hold our little darling."

"We are so happy for you!"

"*Ladies!* What is going on in here? I thought I told you to attend to business." The manager stood in the open doorway.

Even Mrs. Stone's pinched mouth couldn't quell their joy as the women linked arms and headed toward their department.

"Stop the chatter at once!" ordered Mrs. Stone.

On break that afternoon, Eulila and Lillian found themselves alone in the dressing room. They were talking quietly about Lillian's good news. Eulila stood in front of the full-length mirror and rounded up wandering wisps of hair, tucking each one strategically into her bun.

Lillian stopped her and unraveled the bun. "Why haven't you thought of bobbing your hair, dear?" She combed her fingers through an auburn curl.

"Don't tell me you think long hair is horrible, too."

"No, but short hair has a way of highlighting one's attributes. Or bringing them out." She framed Eulila's face with her hands. "You have striking green eyes and the kindest smile and I love your freckles." Lillian suddenly looked shy. "There is so much substance to you, Eulila, and it's hidden under all this hair."

Lillian's face was so serious, Eulila laughed. "Why, I hate my freckles! Even rubbing lemons on my skin hasn't eradicated them."

"They're beautiful, but if you don't like them, you could always cover them with powder!"

"Now you're really going to get me in trouble with Robert!"

"You might be surprised at how good it makes you feel." Lillian reached into her locker and opened an ornate, silver-plated vanity case. Inside were two spring-loaded receptacles for nickels and dimes, several calling cards clasped in the lid, a niche filled with powder and puff, and a tiny mirror. She picked up the puff, touched it to the powder, and patted her nose. "It makes me feel wonderful!"

Oak's battered face flashed across Eulila's mind. *That son of mine could really use some makeup.* She stifled a giggle at the thought. "My land, child. You don't need makeup. I'd love to have skin like yours — smooth and creamy." She ran a fingertip down her friend's cheek. "You're starting a tan, I see," she said with gentle admonishment in her tone. "Have you been working in your garden without a bonnet?"

"Don't switch subjects," Lillian said, snapping her vanity case shut. She smiled. "Besides, don't you know tanning is good for you?"

"It only brings out more freckles on me." Eulila took the handful of hairpins from Lillian's outstretched palm. "All right. I guess the real reason I haven't bobbed my hair is because my husband would have a fit. Robert doesn't like," Eulila rewound her bun, "change."

"Robert, Robert, Robert! Do you know everyone here wonders if the man really exists? He's never come to any picnics or parties, or even here to the store. If I didn't know you better, I'd say you'd made him up so you wouldn't have to make any decisions at all!"

Eulila put her hands to her warm cheeks. "Why, of course my husband exists! What a pot of nonsense! I've never — "

Lillian grinned. "Well, if the man *really* exists," here she looked pointedly at the older woman, "what could he do, once the deed's over? Why don't you test this husband of yours? Let us go to JazzBaby Bobs right now!"

"Oh, Lil, I couldn't — "

"You *are* capable of making decisions on your own, aren't you?"

"Well — "

"Good! Come on, then. Robert will love it when he sees you." Lillian took Eulila's arm. "Besides, you can always grow it back if he doesn't."

Eulila pulled against Lillian as desperation escaped her lips. "Wait, I recently read that a man suicided because his wife had bobbed her hair."

"He had to have been insane in the first place, if that was true. But, not everything you read in the papers is true, now is it?"

Eulila sighed, then shrugged. Resolutely, she held out her elbow. Lillian tugged the woman through the Fair Store and onto the day-lit street. Eulila didn't know whether to laugh or scream, but within moments she was sitting in a barber's chair with a sheet draped over her shoulders.

"Bob it!" cried Lillian, gleefully.

The hairdresser looked at Eulila for permission, and then proceeded after her tentative nod. Each snipped strand of auburn hair was carefully laid next to its sisters on her lap. They would be sold for wigs. Ten minutes later, she was whisked to the back of the room where a sink waited. (Ma'am, if you'll just lean back, I'll make sure the chair doesn't topple.) Her hair was washed and conditioned. (That lovely smell is cocoanut oil, ma'am.) Brushed . . . (A hundred strokes a night, ma'am, will keep this cap sleek and shiny!) And before she knew it, she was back in front of the mirror.

The hairdresser brought out an extremely large contraption with a wooden handle that blew hot air all over Eulila's new bob. At least once, he had to put it down as it overheated. When it was dry, he ran a brush through her hair, whipped the sheet off with a flourish, and smiled broadly. "There you go, ma'am. Bob's your uncle — it's done!" While Lillian cooed her pleasure, a stranger looked back from the mirror. "Next time, ma'am, we'll try a Marcel permanent wave?"

My land! What have I done?

Chapter Four

Colorado Avenue was part of Oak's route. One block south of Main Street, it used to be the original business section of the pioneer town, but now hosted the fire department with its tall hose tower, City Hall and its jailhouse, hotels such as the Melrose and the regal St. Regis, several automobile stores, and liveries, and a few residences. The Evan Treeces lived on the corner of Seventh and Colorado, east of Martin's Funeral Home.

Oak's lip had receded and he'd been attempting to whistle "Ain't We Got Fun?" At Second and Colorado he gave up. Through Hayashi Barber Shop's plate glass window, he watched Mrs. Kotono Hayashi wrap a steaming towel around the face of a gentleman reclining in a barber chair. His Florsheim shoes jerked upward a little as she did. The Japanese lady had been the first woman in western Colorado to get a barber's license. She worked out front, in the barbershop, while her husband ran the pool hall in back.

"Tendewberrymud!" called the woman as Oak tossed a paper through the door.

"You're welcome!"

After delivering New World Café's paper, Oak headed to the LaCourt Hotel, at Second and Main. It was the fanciest hotel in town. William Buthorn, the proprietor, knew how to make his guests feel like royalty. He generally greeted newcomers in a tuxedo and threw theme parties that made a crowd forget their troubles. His "Hobo" party in January had been a hit, so the *Sentinel* reported. It was probably written by Dalton, Oak thought wryly.

He got excited thinking about his meeting with Dalton in a few short minutes. He dropped off a stack of newspapers with Otto Bugg, the hotel's clerk.

Finishing up all but one of his deliveries, Oak rehearsed what he would say to Dalton Trumbo. He cleared his throat and tried talking deeper, more mature. His voice cracked and he gave up. There was just no improving himself. The man would have to take him as he was.

The dangling bell clanged over the entrance. Robert automatically thought *customer*. He looked up from the paperwork he was working on at the counter. Standing in front of the door, en masse, was the Jones family. Their accumulated breadth blocked out the daylight.

John Jones was at least six-foot, five-inches tall, not including his pompous hair. His girth nearly matched his height. He was a preacher in town, though Robert had never asked which church. He was afraid the man would invite him to visit in his smooth, southern tenor, and Robert would have to tell him what he thought about God. Jones may or may not have been a good preacher, but perhaps he was an astute one. He had never extended an invitation.

Next to Jones stood his wife, Mary. She was nearly as tall as her husband, but beanpole thin. Robert had once read about a stick insect that takes its coloring from its surroundings. Mary may well be its cousin for she blended in with her family so well, one had to look twice to see her outline. Robert had no clue what the woman sounded like as she never opened her mouth, at least around him.

"Beryl! Waldine! Lamort! Covina! Susie! Mind your mannahs, ya heah?" Stair-step children, from ages six to ten, moved closer to their parents. If that was possible.

Robert often wondered how Susie, the littlest, got blessed with a simple name. Maybe her parents thought her short leg, thanks to tuberculosis, was enough of a cross to carry through life. *Kind of them.* Round, sunflower-blue eyes materialized behind her mother's skirt.

In spite of himself, Robert smiled at Susie. "And who's in need of a bicycle today?"

Jones pulled his youngest child from the mass and set her in front. The movement reminded Robert of the pull-apart sweet cake Eulila made recently.

"It's Susie's turn. Can you help her?" He jutted out his massive chin.

Robert had been waiting for this day. The Jones family had come in every month for the last six, each time ordering a bicycle to fit the next shorter family member. They could afford only one bicycle at a time, as tithes permitted. Robert had wondered what he would do when it was Susie's turn. How to accommodate her short leg had often kept him awake at night, refiguring and redesigning. He wanted her bicycle to be just right.

Robert hobbled to the counter. He foraged for a piece of paper, a pencil, and a measuring tape and returned to Susie.

"Come closer." Robert could smell milk on the child's breath. It smelled sweet. "Now, I need to measure how tall you are, so stand real still."

With a minimal of movement, Robert took Susie's measurements, including her short leg. She stoically stood gazing at Robert's face the whole time. When he was done, he nodded to her. She brought her small, sticky hands up and pressed each of Robert's cheeks. Without hesitation, she kissed his nose.

Robert stood abruptly. "Yes, well . . ."

Susie waved and then hop-skipped back to her family, reabsorbed into their safety.

"This will take some time. I'll send Evan around when the job's done. When you come to retrieve it, I'll show Susie how to ride. Will that be acceptable?"

Jones took a deep breath and nodded. "That will be — " his bottom lip trembled, "acceptable." He held out his hand. "God has shorely blessed you with a gift, Robert. Mah thanks to you."

Daylight was blocked out again as the family moved through the door. Robert touched his nose thoughtfully.

"Good afternoon, Reverend and Mrs. Jones." Margaret Treece waited until everyone was clear of the entrance before she stepped into the shop.

"And a mawty fine aftanoon to you, miss," intoned John Jones.

Margaret shut the door carefully and waddled to the back of the shop, waving to Robert. She carried a paper-wrapped bundle. Evan had been tightening the spokes on a wheel when his wife approached. His face brightened considerably. She stood on her toes to kiss him on the lips. Robert, who'd been watching, turned away. He was always uncomfortable around public displays of affection. Heck, he had a hard time of it even in his own bedroom.

"Robert, what do you think of this?" Evan held up a knitted blanket. It was lopsided. "For our baby. My Margaret made it herself. Isn't she wonderful?"

He started to pick her up, but she protested saying, "We must be careful, Evan." He looked properly chastised. "I am going to Adam Booker's. What would you like for dinner?"

Evan looked to the ceiling, thinking. "How about your chicken liver omelet? That was delicious."

"Very well. Write down the ingredients and I will ask that new man, Paul Prinster, to help me." As Margaret left, list in hand, the door was held open by a man in a priest's collar.

"Are you the proprietor?" The priest held out his hand. Robert wiped his on his apron before gripping it.

"I'm Robert Miller, yes. How can I help you, Reverend?"

"You're not Catholic, like Evan here, are you?"

Evan had made his way frontward.

"I don't belong to any church. Why do you ask?"

"Catholics know to call me 'Father.'"

"I see. My apologies, Father, er — ?"

"This is Father Nicholas Bertrand, Robert. Father Nick is our new priest at St. Joe's." He held out his hand and the two men shook.

"It is nice to see you, Evan. Now the reason I'm here is to remind all business owners on Main Street about the chamber of commerce meeting tonight at seven. Bill Buthorn will be placing on the table a proposition to change the name of Main Street to Broadway."

"I'd heard about that. Why in tarnation would he suggest such a thing?"

"Well, some feel Grand Junction should be different. Every other town in the west has a Main Street, and Bill thinks changing our Main Street to Broadway would make Grand Junction stick out, bring in more people." The priest's blue-green eyes twinkled as if he found the notion improbable. "Seems quite a few agree with him. Come tonight and have your say, Robert." He looked at Evan. "Will we see you this afternoon, Evan?"

"As always." He never missed Confession.

Oak had delayed delivering his father's paper on purpose. Not only had he ignored his father's order to work in the garden before the banquet last night, his little fracas with Dugger had made him miss his curfew. Anxiety trickled through his veins as he walked slowly toward Miller Bicycle Shop. He'd put off the consequences long enough.

When the door shut behind the priest, Robert perused the flyer Father Nick had left. He followed Evan back to his workstation. "You'd think people had better things to do than to *re-do* what's already been done proper enough!" He reached down and stroked Slugged, who arched his back against Robert's peg leg. "I think I'll skip the meeting. You're welcome to go, if you want." The bell clanged again. "Rather busy today, Evan." Robert turned and his face soured. "You!"

Oak met his father at the counter. Pulling out the last paper, he held it out. "About last night, sir, I'm sorry."

Robert snatched the newspaper from his son's hand and slammed it down on the counter. "I didn't want to say anything in front of your mother or Grace, but you're going to hear from me now, young man.

"When the doctor brought you into this world eighteen years ago, I never thought I'd wish he hadn't. I'm damn close, now. This is the last time you will disappoint me, Oak. You ever disobey me again, you will find yourself out of my house and on your ear!" Robert whacked Oak hard on the side of his head.

Shocked, Oak felt tears sting his eyes. His father had never hit him before. "Yes, sir." He glanced at Evan, who looked away, shaking his head.

Oak ran out of the shop. He struggled to retain a calm public face as he headed to his meeting. It was no use. He couldn't let Dalton see him like this. He slipped into the alley behind the Majestic Theatre to get control.

How dare he hit me like that? The man who hates violence! Ha! And Evan saw it all. Humiliation finally broke the floodgates. Oak leaned his head against the brick wall and hit it over and over.

He was rubbing his sleeve across his eyes when he heard a commotion nearby, followed by a shriek. Sniffing, he walked deeper into the alley until he came to a corner leading to a wide space behind the Odd Fellows building. Familiar voices came from around the corner. Oak peeked and saw Margaret Treece surrounded by Dugger and his pals. Margaret's groceries littered the ground and her dress was torn at the sleeve.

"Seems to me, boys, we have a damsel in distress. Wait, make that a *retard* in distress. You are a retard, aren't you? Isn't she, boys?"

Hal and Chas joined Dugger in circling Margaret and jeering into her face.

"Stop crying! Only *real* people get to cry, right boys? No use calling for your stupid husband, either. The fool! He isn't here to protect you, now is he?"

Oak stepped into view. "No, but I am."

"Oak!" Margaret made a move toward him, but Dugger stopped her with a fist to her abdomen. Oak heard a whoosh of air. Margaret bent over double.

"Where *you* going, retard?"

With a guttural roar, Oak threw himself at Dugger.

"Ha! More fun for us, right boy — !"

Dugger's face registered surprise as he hit the ground hard. He held his arms over his face, crying out as Oak pummeled him. Margaret, struggling to stand up straight, begged for him to stop.

Oak, his fury finally spent, stood over Dugger, heaving. Dugger's features were bloodied and swollen.

"Who's the retard now? Get up and fight, you panty-waist!" Oak nudged Dugger's leg, but he didn't move. He heard a noise behind him and Oak whirled around. Hal and Chas had frozen in mid-flight. They stared at him as Oak raised his fists. "That was too easy, *boys.* I have a lot more where that came from, believe me."

Hal and Chas disappeared around the corner.

Oak's ears were ringing with adrenalin. "Come on, Margaret. We need to get you to Evan." Her face was drained of color and she clutched her midsection. They left Dugger unconscious on the ground.

Within minutes, they staggered into the bicycle shop, a group of bystanders peering into the windows. Oak didn't need to explain something was terribly wrong. Robert pulled out the chair in front of his desk, while Evan ran to look for a doctor. Several had offices in the Grand Valley Bank Building. "Hang on, my darling!" Evan had encouraged.

Robert and Oak waited together, without speaking. The uncomfortable silence was punctuated by Margaret's frequent groans. Oak nudged his shoulder under her arm to support her and hoped the doctor would get here soon. She looked bad.

"I thank you, Oak," she whispered.

"Don't talk, Margaret. Rest."

Robert picked up one of Oak's hands and looked at his battered knuckles. "Did you have to use violence? Only fools fight."

Oak jerked his hand back. "Then I'm a fool." He snorted. "You should talk!"

Robert looked down. "I-I shouldn't have done that."

"Yeah? Tell it to Sweeney."

Robert's face hardened. Oak's knuckles began to ache.

"Please." Margaret fainted into Oak's arms. He was trying to revive her when the doctor arrived. Father and son moved quickly aside. Oak saw a smear of blood on the chair as Margaret was lifted and carried to the doctor's automobile, waiting at the curb. Oak took out his handkerchief and quietly wiped the blood away.

"He's taking her to St. Mary's Hospital," Evan explained. "May I?"

"Of course. I'll clean up." Robert laid a hand on his helper's arm. "Evan, I'm sorry."

"I'm glad your boy was there. There's no telling what condition my wife would be in if he wasn't." Robert said nothing as Evan patted Oak on the back. "Would you contact the authorities? The doctor suggested it."

"I'll do it." Oak couldn't wait to escape. He didn't have to go far to find the police chief. As he jerked open the shop door, Bert Watson was just reaching the doctor's automobile. He stuck his head in the open window and spoke to the doctor. Evan climbed into the back seat, next to his wife. After a brief interchange, the doctor sped away.

When Bert saw Oak, he said, "Got here as soon as I heard. Fella ran into Mesa Drug with the news. Anything you can tell me about the perp, Miller? Say, where you going, young man?"

Oak had started to run. *Damn! Dalton.*

❦

"What have you done, Eulila?" Mrs. Stone looked a shade green. "You, of all people, I would have thought —"

Eulila was dazed but happy, surrounded by second floor employees. She stroked her hair, enjoying the satiny feel of it.

"Mrs. Miller, may I please have a word with you?"

Eulila turned around. Standing behind her was the owner of the Fair Store, William Moyer. As usual, his arms were folded across his chest and his polished shoes angled outward. A yellow carnation decorated his suit's lapel. His balding head was tilted slightly; a gentle face benign around muskrat eyes, which were magnified behind hypermetropic lenses. A bristly toothbrush mustache fringed his lips.

"Now she's in for it!" Lazuli shushed Fluff.

Eulila smiled. "What do you think, William? Isn't it delightful?" She took Moyer's hands in hers and turned her head to the left and right.

"Breathtaking, my dear. It's about time."

"You're a dear!" She kissed the man's cheek.

"Oh!" Mrs. Stone did an about-face and stalked away, her back stiff.

William Moyer's eyes followed her. "Excuse me, ladies. I have a fire to put out." The diminutive man calmly followed his eldest and longest employed friend. He found the woman in a mirrored changing room, picking up dresses that customers had tried on. "Mildred — "

She spoke to his reflection. "Am I the only one who sees how important tradition is, Mr. Moyer?"

Moyer picked up a dress Mrs. Stone had missed. He held it up. "This is the *new* tradition. Shapeless dresses, raised hemlines, flattened chests, rolled stockings — "

"Makeup, tweezed eyebrows, trousers instead of culottes — Mr. Moyer, the world has gone mad!"

"To some it would appear so."

"What about our hard work? Remember the 'Gay Nineties?' Only a few short years ago, family and country were fraught with divorce and corruption. We," she pounded her bird-like chest, "restored order."

"You give our efforts too much credit. God is the only one who brings order out of chaos. We only help Him out once in a while."

"Mr. Moyer," Mrs. Stone wrung her hands, "there's been too much change lately!"

"Change is good. Life should be a progressive thing; strong and vital, carving mankind with bold dreams and new horizons."

"Yes, but — "

"You want to hold on to what's familiar, Mildred, but when life pools too long in one place, it grows stagnant." Moyer patted the woman's shoulder. "I'm afraid our traditions have outstayed their welcome."

Mrs. Stone pulled her shoulder away and shook her head. "No."

Moyer's voice was gentle. "It's inevitable, Mildred. Take comfort, my dear. We have done our best with the times that were handed us. Why don't we let this new generation have the same privilege?"

"Lord, help us."

"I'm sure He does. Quite often."

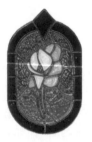

Chapter Five

It was a rubbery walk into the bicycle shop after work. Eulila's husband didn't say anything when he saw his wife, but the grim set of his mouth had her heart pounding as she drove them home.

She hated the fear she felt when Robert was like this. It was happening more often. For years Robert had soaked up anger like a sponge, and now he seemed close to the saturation point. Eulila worried her husband might soon wring a tsunami of bitterness over his family. Would the Millers withstand the drenching?

"Robert?"

"Yes, Eulila?"

"About my hair — "

"The subject is closed."

"No, it wouldn't do to discuss it, would it?" Eulila pulled the brake hard in front of the house. "You've already made up your mind."

Robert got out of the Ford and headed to the backyard.

Dinner was quiet.

Grace spooned Tomato Toast into her mouth without taking her eyes off her mother's hair. She was sure this was the last straw. It was the end of her family! Her foot tapped nervously.

Thoughts whirled restlessly around in Oak's mind, too. His father, Lazuli, Margaret, and the missed meeting with Dalton all became one confusion of doubt. He nursed his bruised knuckles.

Eulila could barely eat, glancing often at the empty chair at the head of the table. She'd known Robert wouldn't be pleased with her hair, yet she'd gone ahead and bobbed it. Whatever had possessed her? Should she find Robert and beg his forgiveness? No, this wasn't about her. If it was, she could change it. Instead, she did what she always did when Robert was unreasonable: she prayed.

After the kitchen chores were done, Robert came in, sweat and dirt covering his face and overalls like he'd had a free-for-all with the garden. Oak and Grace, seeing his mood, escaped to the covered front porch.

As usual, Oak scanned the *Sentinel* and studied the best-written articles. Grace picked up her jump rope and began a ditty. When the argument started inside, she jumped harder.

> *Our mother, our father, had a rotten day,*
> *And tonight, they're going to fight*
> *And this is what they'll say —*

"Grace, would you mind doing that on the sidewalk? You're jostling my paper."

Grace stopped and looked at her brother. "Don't you care that they may get a divorce?"

"It won't come to that."

"The Buellers got a divorce, and so did the Garolas. And so did — "

"The Millers will not. Stop being pessimistic." That was a word he'd found in yesterday's best article. Oak rolled the word over his tongue one more time as the din in the house got louder.

"You just wait." Grace started jumping rope again, pounding even harder on the wooden porch.

> *Oak and Grace sitting in a well,*
> *Listening to their parents yell . . .*

Oak sighed and turned his back on his sister. It grew silent inside the house. "See? Everything has settled down. You worry too much. Pastor Jim says that's a lack of faith."

> *First comes war, then animosity*
> *Then comes divorce,*
> *Just like I said there'd be.*

"Enjoying the evening?"

Oak looked up and started. Dalton Trumbo stood on the sidewalk. "Could be better." He looked at his sister. "Dalton, meet Grace. Sis, this is Dalton Trumbo."

Grace continued jumping, but said "Hi."

Dalton saluted her, then turned to Oak. "I heard what happened to Margaret Treece. Shame. Bert found Dugger unconscious in the alley. McClintock already has a story worked up for tomorrow.

"I also heard you were the one that roughed up that high hat. I don't usually hold to solving problems that way, but I'm sure you did what you had to."

That was more understanding than what Oak's father had given him. "Have you heard how she's doing?"

Dalton shook his head. "Won't know until tomorrow."

"Oh. Where you heading?"

"Earlene Hospital." He indicated the next block, where the small, private hospital was. "Jack and Wanda Dill were driving a team of horses down Whitewater Hill, lost control, and crashed at the bottom. I'm going to get the facts for a story. Care to come along?"

"I'm keen to the idea." Oak went to the screen door and called, "Mother, I'll be back soon." He didn't wait for a reply. As he and Dalton walked away, Grace started a new song.

> *Mother and Father sitting in a tree*
> *How I wish they were ki-i-ssing . . .*

Earlene Hospital was a long, two-story bungalow nestled between the tenth and eleventh blocks of Chipeta. Many Grand Junction residents had been born or died there, and since a part of the complex was a rest home, some were living out their later years there, as well.

Oak and Dalton inquired about the injured couple at the nurse's station just inside the entrance. They were informed the doctor was checking on them, but it wouldn't be long before visitors were allowed in.

Dalton led Oak to the covered patio where a few recovering patients and elderly enjoyed the sunset's glow. The young men sat down on a couple of green Adirondack chairs. Oak nodded at a man whose leg was encased in plaster of Paris and stretched out on an extension of his wheelchair. He returned an agonized smile. Oak was thankful he had never broken a bone.

"One must wait until evening to see how splendid the day has been." Dalton rested against the slanted back of the Adirondack, locking his fingers behind his head.

"Poetic." Oak always found it hard to relax in an Adirondack chair. He shuffled around until he found a comfortable position.

"Will Rogers always is."

"I'd say *this* day has been a far cry from 'splendid.'" Oak closed his eyes.

"I'd say I'm sorry, but I'm not the sentimental type. Tomorrow's another day. Since you missed our meeting today, why don't we have it while we wait?"

Oak's eyes opened. He still had a chance at Dalton's beat!

Dalton jumped right in. "Why do you want to be a reporter?"

"I don't just want to 'be a reporter.' I want to make a difference."

"How do you propose to do that?"

"Like the great newspaper columnists in New York, I'll educate the public on life and current affairs. I'll investigate, then report the truth."

"Are you sure people want to hear the truth?"

Oak was nonplussed. "Of course they want to hear the truth. *I* want to."

"Perhaps." Dalton studied Oak's face, until Oak began to fidget. "I'll tell you what, let's share some assignments this week.

"Top of the list is the possible drowning of that paralytic, Roy Johnson. As you may know, he went missing yesterday and is now believed to have met death by drowning in the Gunnison River. It's too dark to start a search party, so we probably won't hear anything new until tomorrow. Why don't you meet me at the *Sentinel*, after church? You go to church?"

Oak nodded. "It will have to be after Sunday dinner, though. Mother insists on attendance."

"One o'clock, then. Be thinking about some angles for our other big assignment: Better Homes and Gardens Week. I'm anxious to see what you're made of."

At that moment, a uniformed nurse came out of the side door and indicated the two men could see the accident victims now. When their interview with the bruised and bandaged couple was done, Dalton walked Oak home. He reminded Oak of their meeting the next day. "Try to avoid any heroics on the way."

The house was quiet when Oak walked in. Everyone's bedroom door was shut, so Oak grabbed a glass of milk and headed to the sleeping porch. He had a big day ahead of him.

When Oak came out of the bathroom the next morning, Grace was leaning against the wall, tapping her foot. She clutched her towel and toothbrush. "I almost had to run and use Sally's toilet, on her back porch! It's freezing outside, Oak. It would be nice if you were a little considerate — "

Oak escaped into Grace's bedroom to change into his Sunday suit. He closed the door on his sister's complaints. *You'd think there was an emergency.*

He'd been up early to deliver Sunday papers. It was the only day of the week that deliveries were in the morning. Oak dressed meticulously, making sure his tie was straight this time. Last Sunday the head elder had yanked it straight, hailing him with warning looks.

Satisfied, Oak allowed his sister (again with the tapping foot!) back in her room. He gravitated toward the delicious aroma coming from the kitchen.

"There's not much time. Eat your omelet," Eulila said as she placed a plate in front of Oak.

He stared it. It reminded him of that beached whale the family had once seen on a visit to the California coast. Only this one was pale yellow. Taking his fork, he pried the omelet open and explored its innards. Chopped onions, bacon, and — green beans! *Mother will stoop to anything to see I get my vegetables.* Separating the beans from the rest, he dug in.

"Delish, Mother," Oak said, quickly dumping the offending green beans into the trash, to be burned in their backyard incinerator. "Think I'll walk to church. Have some things to think about." He kissed his mother's cheek, flushed from cooking over her new electric skillet. "By the way," Oak glanced around to make sure his father wasn't near, "everything okey-dokey here? Er, Grace is worrying again."

"That girl! Your father's moodiness will calm down once he gets used to, well, you know." She touched her hair and a small smile flickered. "Do you like it, Oak?"

"It's the gnat's eyebrows!"

Eulila preened. "You're my favorite son."

"I'm your only son."

"That's beside the point." She scooted another fat omelet onto a plate and called, "Grace, come eat your breakfast!"

After Sunday dinner, where the family was treated to more green beans and Robert's silence, Oak strolled to the *Sentinel* office. Flanking its entrance were two columns, giving the impression one was about to enter a Greek temple. Or at least someplace as special.

The only time Oak had ever entered the front door was to apply as a delivery boy. He picked up his newspapers every day around back, at the loading dock.

The doors closed behind Oak, and he removed his cap. The interior of *The Daily Sentinel* was something to behold. A stained glass skylight solemnly infused the lobby, while chandeliers and a painting of the Grand Mesa on the back wall added to the glamour. Dark paneling lined the walls and painted pillars supported the high ceiling. Flowered runners muffled the polished wooden floors.

A wide oak receptionist's desk spanned the width of the room. Here one filed a classified ad, paid a bill, or perused any back issues that were hardbound and stored under the counter. The receptionist was also the switchboard operator for the *Sentinel.*

Cubbies flanked the west wall, each labeled appropriately: City Desk, News Editor, Society, Advertising. To the right was Marion Fletcher's office, Walter Walker's secretary. You had to go through her to get to the publisher's large corner office. The huge press, located in the basement, pulsed underfoot, the heartbeat of the newsroom. Behind the receptionist's desk were several oak desks, strewn with papers, Royal typewriters, telephones, lamps, and other office flotsam. This was the reporters' area.

Cigarette smoke hung in the air in wispy clouds, emanating from one desk surrounded by several men. All were smoking, with inch-long ashes clinging to their cigarettes. A card game had their attention for the moment, but Oak imagined if the telephone rang with breaking news, they'd scramble to beat each other out the door. Dalton wasn't among them.

Oak saw his raised hand and walked over to a corner desk. He barely looked up when Oak arrived. The spare chair next to the desk was stacked with books, so Oak laid them neatly on the floor and sat down. He was careful not to disturb Dalton, who scribbled furiously on a notebook.

"Help yourself to some java. Warm mine up, while you're at it." He pointed at nothing in particular.

Oak picked up Dalton's cup. Haviland China, Oak noted. Chipped, at that. He wandered around until he found a door marked "Break Room." There, a silver percolator popped and crackled as it finished brewing. Coffee sure smelled good to Oak, but he had never tasted the brew. He reached for the handle, but never got to grasp it. He was crowded out of the vicinity by a clamor of reporters. When he finally reached the percolator again, it was empty.

"Say, can you get another pot going?"

Oak stared at the man. "Um, sure." He had no clue how to get a "pot going." Oak waited until he had left the break room, unplugged the percolator, and then slunk out to Dalton's desk. "All out. Sorry."

Withdrawing his own notebook and pencil from his jacket pocket, he cleared his throat. "So . . ."

Dalton held up a finger and finished his sentence. He reread it, nodded his head, then lifted his eyes to Oak. "Ready to work today?"

"Yup."

"First off, if you are going to be a reporter, you better look like one. Take your jacket off."

Oak folded his jacket neatly on his lap. Dalton reached over and loosened Oak's tie and undid the top button of his dress shirt. After sticking Oak's pencil behind his ear, he said, "Now, roll up your sleeves." Oak did as he was told. "Cigarette?" Oak dangled an unlit cigarette from his mouth. Dalton looked satisfied.

"Okay, here's the scoop. A search party went out early this morning, looking for traces of Johnson. Let's find Chief Watson and pick his brain."

Before they exited the building, Dalton buttoned his shirt, tightened his tie, rolled down his sleeves, put on his jacket, stuck the pencil and notebook in his breast pocket, and donned his hat. Oak followed suit.

They found the police chief at Mesa Drug, sipping coffee by the window and watching passersby. "Hey, Chief, mind if we sit down?" Dalton pulled out a chair without waiting for a response. Oak tentatively pulled out another, expecting Bert to reprimand them for their insolence.

"Trumbo, what bee is in your bonnet today?"

"A drowned one, Chief."

Though Oak didn't recall a waitress asking, two more coffee cups were set on the table and filled. He thanked the waitress — a frilly handkerchief kind of girl — and brought the steaming cup to his lips. He stifled the grimace that welled up.

"Try some sugar." Dalton pushed a ceramic sugar bowl his way.

"Do *you* use sugar?"

"Nope."

"Neither do I. I – I just brushed my teeth and you know how baking soda makes everything taste." He took another delicate sip. "Mmm. Much better." Bert and Dalton exchanged knowing smirks.

Dalton quickly got to business. "Chief, before we get to Johnson, can you tell us who was jailed this weekend?"

"The usual. Painted ladies, rumrunners, still-sitters, a couple of whisper sisters, partiers. Someone ran into the light pole on the corner of Twelfth and Grand sometime Friday night. Nearly knocked it on its face. Perp left the scene, but he shouldn't be too hard to locate. Had to have smashed his radiator grill like an accordion. He'll be found, don't you worry."

"Probably that washout, Dugger," Oak said. "One day he'll kill someone with his wild driving. If he doesn't kill some innocent woman first."

Dalton snorted. "Dugger thinks the sun comes up just to hear him crow. I never met anyone who was as ugly on the inside as he was on the outside."

"He's a bad sort, all right." Bert rubbed his clean-shaven face. "He was released yesterday. That lawyer father of his posted bail. We picked up his friends, who aren't so lucky. They're still cooling their heels behind bars."

"They all deserve to be tarred and feathered!"

"No doubt, Oak." Dalton cleared his throat. "Well, Chief, what's the up-to-date on Roy Johnson?"

"Still not much. Just got word that J. H. Yeager found Johnson's horse in a thicket a distance from the Billings cabin, some three miles above the Gunnison River dam. Johnson must have rode the horse into the swift running water, not realizing the river was still high."

Dalton directed Oak to take notes while Bert gave details about Johnson's worried parents and friends; how a general alarm was sounded Friday night, a search party was put together early Saturday morning, with Lions Club members and Rotarians asked to join; that horse tracks led into the river at one point; remnants of someone's lunch, probably Johnson's, was found at the Billings cabin; and that downstream, horse tracks led from the river to some nearby bushes, where its reins were caught.

"We figure Johnson was washed away, while the horse made it to safety."

"No body yet?"

Bert shook his head.

"We'll check back later. Thanks, Chief."

"Yep." The man's gaze flicked to the street scene. He sighed. "The world don't make sense, some days."

"This from a hardboiled thick skin such as yourself? Don't go soft on us, Bert. Someone's got to keep his head above water. No pun intended."

"None taken. You boys stay out of trouble."

The two young men left the drug store after paying at the cash register. They left a penny tip for the waitress.

They walked back to the *Sentinel* office to write the story. Dalton let Oak type it up while he wrote a short piece about the light pole incident.

Taking five pieces of onionskin paper and placing carbon paper neatly between each page, Oak started typing:

Missing Man Believed To Be Drowned
Roy Johnson, a Paralytic, Has Been Missing Since
Friday Morning — Horse's Tracks Led Into River

When Oak had finished, Dalton carefully pulled the pages out of the old Royal and began to read. "Nice job. Will Rogers isn't the only poet." Dalton read aloud, "'His mount was his faithful companion on frequent long rides to the west and south from this city.' Good enough to hand in, as is. I'll let the desk know you get the byline." He gave Oak one of the copies, "for your file." Oak was pleased.

Dalton clapped him on the back and said, "Well done, my boy!" He told Oak to meet him at his desk the next morning to begin work on the piece about Better Homes and Gardens Week.

At home, he took the porch steps in one leap.

"Where have you been?"

Oak's good spirits took a tumble. His father sat in the shadows, holding a glass of lemonade.

"Working, sir."

"I thought you Christians were supposed to rest on the Sabbath." Robert sipped his drink.

"Normally I would, but there was breaking news."

"So, now you are a big-talking reporter. His Highness, the all-important *reporter*."

Oak wondered what was in his lemonade. His father was more acerbic than usual. Whatever his reason, Oak was tired of his treatment. "Why are you such a bitter man? You should go to church. Maybe some good preaching would crack that hard heart of yours."

"God hasn't done me any favors so far. No reason to expect a change in the routine."

"You should raise your expectations, sir." Oak slammed the front screen on his way in.

Chapter Six

Monday morning Robert unlocked the shop's front door, a job usually handled by Evan. As he opened the cash register he wondered if Evan would make it in. A moment later, his helper arrived.

"I'm sorry I'm late. I had to wait for Lillian to arrive." Evan donned his apron.

"Oh?" Robert picked up a half-filled bottle of milk he'd brought from home and poured some into the cat's bowl. Slugged twirled clumsily around Robert's peg leg until the bowl was set down. He slurped the treat noisily.

"Margaret lost the baby," Evan said quietly.

Robert sighed. "I don't know what to say. It's a tragedy."

"Yes, it is."

"You seem to be, well, handling it. Admirable."

Evan bent down to pet Slugged. The cat's whiskers were wet and strangely comforting. He fought tears. "Yes. No matter what, God is still on His throne."

"Eh?"

The bell over the entrance jangled. Robert immediately turned toward the door. He'd ask Evan about his comment later.

Percival Harrison reminded Robert of a hound dog: loose jowls, double-bagged eyes, and a morose mouth. His voice was normally tranquil — a good fit for his profession as assistant at Martin's Funeral Home. At the moment he didn't sound very tranquil. "Is somebody going to help me or am I going to stand here until the sun goes down?"

Robert sighed deeply. *Already a Monday.*

"I'll be right with you, Mr. Harrison." Robert turned to Evan. "Will you cross-check my measurements for Susie Jones' bicycle?"

Evan took a crumpled handkerchief out of his pants pocket and blew his nose. "Right away."

"I say, do you want my business or not?"

"Certainly." Robert walked up front and picked up a notebook and pencil. "How may I help you?"

Percival looked suspiciously over Robert's shoulder to Evan. "May I speak to you alone?" He lowered his voice. "I'm in a bit of trouble."

"My shop hand is discrete."

Percival looked doubtful.

"Why don't you tell me the problem?"

"I'm afraid I had an accident this weekend. Oh, nothing big, mind you, just a mis-meeting between my vehicle and, er, well, a light post. I'm afraid I made a mess of things as I left without reporting it. Not that I won't send along some money to repair it, mind you. The trouble, you see . . .that is . . .now see here, young man — I just can't drive anymore! I've been having these dizzy spells for a while . . ."

"Ah."

"I'm told you have, well, a way with these situations."

By now, the bags under Percival Harrison's eyes had slunk halfway down his cheeks. A more melancholy man Robert had never seen. He felt sorry for him. "Let me think on this for a couple of days, Mr. Harrison. I'll see what I can come up with. Allow me to take some measurements." After Robert put down his pad, he walked Percival to the door.

"You'll not tell anyone?" Percival spoke low.

"Your secret is safe with me. Stop by on Thursday. I should have something worked up by then."

Percival looked over Robert's shoulder. "No one is to know, you hear?"

Robert shook his head after the man had left.

⚘

"How is Margaret, Evan?" Robert held on to the bicycle tire while Evan tweaked a bolt on the frame.

"She's recovering. Lillian Gesberg stayed with her every day since she lost the — our baby."

Robert hung his head. "I'm sorry."

"I am as well. It was a boy. The body is at Callahan's until the funeral. Today Margaret and I will visit Bannister Furniture to pick out the coffin. That's if I may get the time off?"

"All you need. Did Watson get the criminals who did this?"

Evan grunted as he tightened the bolt. "Bert had them in custody, but Dugger's father bailed him out."

"Unfair!" Robert spat the word out. After a moment he asked, "Where will the burial be?"

Evan shrugged. "Margaret would like him lain in her flowerbed under the kitchen window. I'd rather it be in the cemetery. What if we moved?"

Robert nodded. He took out a rag and rubbed at the excess grease on the tire rim until it sparkled. "Evan?"

"Yes?"

"What did you mean by, 'God is still on His throne'?"

"Are you sure you want to know?"

Robert hesitated. "Yes."

"I'm a man of faith, Robert. It colors the way I see things. Losing my son is a tragedy, one of countless tragedies that have occurred on this earth since its time began. Like everyone who loses someone — or something — precious, I grieve. But my comfort comes from knowing that God still sits on His throne."

"Why does that comfort you?"

"Well, you see, Robert, because He reigns, I will see my son again."

That evening, several visitors ate together at the Treece cottage. Eulila, Robert, Oak, and Grace Miller and Lillian Gesberg sat around the small, but neat, living room. Their near-empty dishes were balanced on their knees.

Eulila and Grace had made the evening meal: roasted chicken, mashed potatoes, and sliced tomatoes — nothing that would upset the digestive system. Lillian had brought dessert, an Orange Pekoe Mousse.

Soft greens accented the walls and floor, and lacy curtains framed the windows throughout the dwelling. Secondhand furniture, covered in bright, homemade afghans, was carefully placed to give the room dimension. The scent of rain floated through the open windows.

Margaret rested on the davenport, a hand-crocheted blanket lain across her lap. Her eyes were rimmed in red. Evan sat close by, holding her hand.

Oak sat cross-legged on the floor, eating a second helping of everything. Robert looked uncomfortable, perched on the overstuffed chair arm, above his wife. He hated visiting people, especially when a death was involved. And the drive home in the rain was bound to be tedious. He'd suffer through it for Evan and Margaret's sake, at least a little while longer.

Grace began picking up the dirty dishes, bringing them into the kitchen for washing. Lillian fluttered around, filling cups with coffee and the somber room with chitchat. As she passed Margaret, she tucked her blanket closer. The room had gotten chilly.

"Mags, you should have eaten more. You need to keep up your strength."

"I'm sorry, Lillian. Maybe tomorrow."

Lillian gave Margaret a worried look. "Evan, I love the story of how you and Mags met. Why don't you tell the Millers?"

Robert sighed loudly. Eulila looked up with a warning stare. "Oh, that would be nice," she said. She moved a little closer to the edge of her seat. "I'm partial to a good love story."

Evan got up and closed the living room window, shutting out the moist breeze. The cuckoo clock chimed eight times. He returned to his seat. "I wasn't the best of men before I met Margaret. I'm ashamed to admit my purpose for being in Whitman Park that spring evening wasn't for a daily constitutional. I was preparing to bed down for the night.

"When I graduated high school, my father kicked me out of our home on Orchard Mesa. He had enough mouths to feed, he said. I knew the day had been coming, but I'd not prepared for it. I had no home, no job, and no future.

"Weeks passed while I looked for a job and place to stay. Jobs were scarce, lodging scarcer. Each night I'd take my one meal at the Catholic soup kitchen and then head to Whitman Park to spend the night. I'd sleep under a bush to avoid the authorities.

"The evening I met Margaret, she was sitting on the bench nearest my bush. Impatient at first, I walked around, waiting for her to leave so I could go to bed. I stopped to read the memorial of Marcus B. Whitman. Between 'his heroic transcontinental ride' and 'saved the Northwest to the United States,' I glanced at the girl and became transfixed." Evan reached over and caressed a strand of blonde hair.

"The sunset shone all around her still figure in a glowing, otherworldly way. I approached her, but she seemed in a trance. She didn't move, even when I sat down next to her. I waited and eventually she turned to me and asked, 'Did you hear it?'"

"I'd been listening, you see." Margaret's gaze was far in the past.

"To what, Mags?" asked Lillian.

"A beautiful voice. It made me cry."

"What did it say, Mags?"

Grace leaned against the kitchen doorjamb, a dishtowel in her hand, looking intently at Margaret. Oak had stopped eating sensing something profound was about to be said.

Margaret's eyes shimmered. "It said, 'Joy is sorrow overcome and transformed.'"

"Astounding!" Eulila said, looking up at her husband. She was surprised to see him listening.

"I knew this lovely vision had to be mine, yet I had nothing to offer her but my adoration," Evan said as he squeezed his wife's hand. "Fortunately, the next week, Robert had hired me, and soon afterward Miss Margaret Templeton became Mrs. Evan Treece."

"What do you think the, er, voice meant, Margaret?" Grace had come in and knelt by the davenport. "'Joy is sorrow overcome and transformed.'"

"I think I know," Lillian said. "When Art lost Ruth to scarlet fever, he was beside himself with grief. To find peace, he went to his special cave.

"Growing up, he and his brothers explored the Gunnison River and its bluffs, and one day they found this little cave. It overlooks a part of the river that curves inward, with the bluffs blocking the view to the east and west.

"His brothers didn't think much of it, but it became a refuge for Art. Being the youngest, he'd often hide there to escape his older brothers.

"He hiked there many times to grieve Ruth's death. He'd lean against the cave's opening and watch the river move along its path, the way it had for millennia. As it curved around the bend and out of sight, he thought of where the river had come from and where it was going. Even though he saw only a part of it, he knew its waters had been born and were emptied out far beyond his limited view.

"Maybe he heard your 'beautiful voice,' Mags, but one day he had a revelation. Maybe life was like the segment of river before him; Ruth had been born and traversed this world for a short time. Now her spirit had been carried around the bend, emptying into the everlasting arms of the Lord."

Margaret sighed.

"So Ruth — and the baby — are not really gone, just somewhere else?"

"That's right, Grace, someplace wonderful," replied Lillian. "Now who wants a bit of my lovely mousse?" She bustled into the kitchen, with Grace following, to dish up dessert.

"Evan, did you pick out a casket today?" asked Robert.

"We did. Ollie Bannister showed us the best caskets he had. I told him they were beyond our means, but he said it was taken care of. Robert, you didn't pay — ?"

He shook his head. "I wish I could."

"Then who?"

"It is beautiful, too." Lillian had returned and handed Evan a plate. "A four-tiered lid, adorable lamb handles, and a metal plate that says 'Our Angel.' I liked the one that said 'Our Darling' better, but Margaret was taken with the other."

Margaret began to sniff. "Our little angel," she cried woefully.

Robert insisted on leaving Margaret's comfort to Evan and Lillian. After quick goodbyes, he piled his family into the car. While Oak and Robert drew the window curtains and tightened them against the rain, Grace curled up in the back seat. She had dozed off by the time they climbed in. Oak drew his jacket closer around his face and tried not to shiver. Suddenly he was very tired and looked forward to his bed. Eulila steered them toward home.

As the rain fell, Robert watched the wipers tic-tac back and forth across the windshield. "Do you think Margaret really heard a voice?"

"Yes. I think the Lord spoke to her."

Robert snorted.

"It's true. He speaks to all of us."

"Well, He doesn't speak to me."

"He does, Robert. You've chosen not to listen."

"Why should I?" he muttered.

Chapter Seven

Early Tuesday morning Oak began the assignment Dalton had given him the day before — to find human-interest stories connected with Grand Junction's annual Better Homes and Gardens Week.

This was part of the national "Better Homes in America" campaign, started three years before in New York through the efforts of Mrs. William Brown Meloney. Towns and communities across the country conducted demonstrations to better educate families and businesses and help raise the living conditions.

Calvin Coolidge, in his radio address that week, encouraged all Americans to join in. "The American home is the source of our national well-being," he'd said. "From the true home there emerges respect for the rights of others and the habit of cooperating for worthy ends."

Merchants had been encouraged to advertise during the preceding Thrift Week, Ice Cream Week, Canned Food Week, and Music Week. The message of better living was praised from storefronts — where sales signs were plastered, to pulpits — where "Cleanliness is next to Godliness" was sermonized each Sunday. *The Daily Sentinel* had given extensive space to all aspects of home improvement: new indoor decorating tips, the most up-to-date kitchen and bathroom designs, and the benefits of owning your own home.

Oak had no trouble finding leads in a town abuzz with activity. His first stop was on the corner of Eleventh and

Gunnison, just west of Dalton's house. The Griffith home had been remodeled and was offering tours. On arrival, Oak was proudly led through rooms showcasing model furnishings, ventilation, lighting, window dressings, and flooring.

In the master bedroom, Oak was introduced to something called a "Murphy Bed," which could be tucked away, fully made, into its closet. Another bedroom had a "day bed," which could be folded up into a davenport to allow more room.

The kitchen was particularly appetizing to Oak. Using the new "Buck's Sanitary Porcelain Enameled Combination Range," which "never fails to brighten monotonous days for weary mothers and housekeepers," two women baked a constant supply of savory Cheese Fingers made from BE-RO Self-Rising Flour. A General Electric refrigerator was placed in the kitchen rather than on or near the porch as iceboxes normally were, for convenience. Abutting one wall was a magnificent Hoosier Cabinet, and by the sink, "the housewife's dream," a Walker Electric Dishwasher. A sign resting on an easel stated one of the leading hardware stores in town had renovated the kitchen.

After Oak had his fill of Cheese Fingers, he wandered to the bathroom, where he was told in falsetto tones, "bathroom décor was a measure of one's status." The modern "necessity" was hidden and quiet. The porcelain sink and bathtub were rose-colored, one of a vast number of shades to choose from. The floor and walls were tiled and, to Oak's surprise, the towel bars were heated.

He could get used to this, he thought as he stood in front of the seashell-shaped vanity mirror. He examined his reflection and noticed his bruised demeanor was subsiding rather quickly. As he moved away, he realized it was just the soft lighting overhead.

In the living room, the YMCA served tea, while a small band, organized from Grand Junction High School students, played ukuleles enthusiastically, though inartistically.

Oak was impressed. Before he headed to Dr. Bell's house, across the street, he filled several pages of notes.

At 1050 Gunnison Avenue, Dr. Bell's residence showcased updated yards. The back lawn sported a playground with the newest equipment, and on the brick patio Oak watched a demonstration of flower arrangements around the grounds and inside the house to show the beauty that flowers offered. To his question of whether flowers were frivolous in the home, Oak was told that beauty was never frivolous, that it delighted the soul and lifted the spirit. More scribbling.

Time to hit Main Street. The big Electric Ferris Wheel and the Carry-Us-All were spinning happily behind Grand Valley National Bank. Squeals were heard many feet above the heads of pedestrians. A gaily-clad man trumpeted that his rides were the "finest portable rides in the west — the cleanest and most wholesome amusement on earth." A large sign invited all to "COME! COME! COME! See Slim Jim, the Texas acrobat, give a performance on the Ferris wheel each afternoon and evening." Oak made a note to stop by later and see this Slim Jim.

Every store had its sale going. Crown Furniture, with its perpetual "Going out of Business" signs, was booming, while Bannister's touted bedroom suites for $228 at $15 down and $15 a month.

That was something new — those easy little payment plans. Oak thought it was the wave of the future. With credit, all Americans could live better, earlier in life. You could even buy automobiles on credit.

Yowzah! What a crazy idea!

J.C. Penney, Sampliner's, and the Fair Store all had their most fashionable clothes on sale. Their windows were resplendent with tailored suits and lightweight summer dresses. The Fair even had a pretty "Nightingale Girl," on loan from Denver, demonstrating in their window. Every hour she showed the many fine points of quality that were placed in Nightingale Hose. Harold Wolverton had outdone himself in reproducing a woman's boudoir.

Mrs. Atkins, at the Dandy Candy Shop, offered free samples of Necco Wafers, and Van, the Drug Man, was handing out tiny tubes of something called Pepsodent toothpaste. Benge, the Shoe Man, had a sidewalk sale going.

Oak peeked into the cool interior and saw Dalton's father, Orus, using a shoehorn to stuff a woman's foot into a dainty shoe. She looked familiar.

"Now, Mr. Trumbo, these are waaaaay too big!"

"Ma'am, if they were any smaller, you'd . . . "

Oak's stomach rumbled. The Cheese Fingers had worn off, so he decided to stop and eat at Mesa Drug. At the door were bins of different free samples. Each had an advertisement attached.

Knowing his mother and sister would enjoy them, Oak picked up two bars of Woodbury's Facial Soap *(You too, can have a skin you love to touch.)* and for himself, a little bottle of Listerine *(Are you sure about yourself?)*. For Dalton he chose a small pack of Chesterfield Cigarettes *(I'll tell the world they satisfy.)* and for his father, a tiny can of Old Dutch Cleanser *(Cleanliness brings good cheer!)*.

Father could use a little good cheer.

"Hey, toots. What lion attacked you?"

Oak waved to Pansy. "A cowardly one." He wondered if she was still living at Nell Page's. He found a table and after ordering a peanut butter and bacon sandwich and coffee, he pulled out his notebook.

"Do you mind if I join you?"

Oak gulped. "It would be my — "

"Pleasure?" Lazuli sat down in one fluid movement next to Oak and scooted her chair close. Very close. "Do you realize you say that to me all the time? Pleasure."

Oak could feel her breath on his face. "Do I? Silly me. Heh-heh."

"What are you doing?" The girl angled her head so she could read Oak's notes. He covered them with his hands. "No, don't do that." Lazuli gently pried the notes from his fingers and smoothed them against the tabletop. "You write very well."

Suddenly, Oak felt slaphappy all over. "I aim to be the best," he gushed. "I plan to go to the big city and be a crack reporter. Some day."

Lazuli's long blonde eyelashes fluttered with amusement. "In the meantime, you are being a reporter in our *little town*?"

"You know your onions."

She smiled and picked up Oak's hand, peering at the bruises. "That nasty boy!" Her eyes had turned to stone. "I hope he goes to jail and they throw away the key!"

"Isn't he — your boyfriend?" Oak was enjoying the attention his hand was getting.

"Huh! He thinks so."

Lazuli brought Oak's hand to her lips and kissed each bruise tenderly. Oak watched, mesmerized. Those flower-petal lips, those melting eyes —

"Um, I should finish these notes . . . " He pulled his hand away.

"I'm sorry. I've embarrassed you."

He couldn't look at her. "I — "

"Here's your sandwich. Does the little lady want something?" Pansy stepped between Oak and Lazuli, placing his plate in front of him with one hand and topping off his now cold coffee with the other. "Well?" She looked at Lazuli expectantly.

"No, thank you. I really should get back to the Fair, Oak. I'll leave you to your dinner and writing. Are we still on for Friday?"

"I'll pick you up at seven."

Lazuli looked like she wanted to say more, but she shrugged a shy smile and left. Oak watched her cross the street and enter the Fair. He watched the door long after it had shut.

By the time Oak reached the *Sentinel* building, he was loaded down with notes, flyers, free samples, and self-confidence.

"Junction 5-0." The comely receptionist answered the switchboard in a professional tone. She motioned to Oak that he had a message.

While he waited, Oak went through what was now routine: jacket, tie, button, sleeves, pencil. He'd decided to forgo the cigarette. His mother hated the smell.

"I'll connect you right away, ma'am."

"Keeping busy, Millie?" Oak asked when she disconnected. He leaned nonchalantly on his elbow and placed a tube of Pepsodent in front of her.

"And how!" Picking up the toothpaste, she asked, "What's this? Gee, it tastes like mint!"

"That's to make your pearly whites shine. At least that's what I'm told." Oak grinned to show his own set of teeth.

Millie replaced the cap and put the tube in her mesh purse. "You're the limit! Say, got something for you." She scrounged around on her desk. "Here it is! It's from Dalton." She offered the reporter's message as though it was caviar on a silver platter.

Oak glanced over the note. *Gone to a funeral. Walker liked your article. Dalton.*

"Better get to work. Got lots to write before deliveries." Oak whistled his way to an empty desk, sensing Millie's curious eyes following him. He was feeling on top of the world. Maybe Dalton would be back before he finished. Slipping the requisite four carbons between five sheets of paper, Oak got to work.

. . . making a sweet and wholesome family life available to all by modern methods and inventions for homemakers of moderate means.

Oak reread his article. Satisfied, he carefully pulled the copies out of the Royal and distributed them to the proper desks, one being Dalton's. He kept a copy for his "file." When he got one.

He had hoped Dalton would make an appearance before he had to do deliveries, but he was disappointed. Leaving the pack of Chesterfields on the reporter's desk, Oak headed to the dock.

Calvary Cemetery was located near the Municipal and Masonic Cemeteries on Orchard Mesa. High above, on Reservoir Hill, George Crawford's tomb overlooked the pioneer town he'd founded in 1881. On the other side of the hill, the Gunnison River carved its way to the confluence of the Colorado River.

In the shade of a cottonwood Robert, Eulila, Grace, Art Gesberg and his wife, Lillian, milled around, waiting for the ceremony to begin. Several yards away, William Moyer stood in the sun, sorrow in his stance. Mr. Callahan, the funeral director, and an overall-clad man holding a shovel stood at a respectable distance.

Margaret sat in front; her wheelchair was manned by her mother, a woman who looked only a few years older than her daughter. Evan, his parents, and Margaret's father pressed close around her.

A tiny casket rested next to a square hole in the ground, a spray of calla lilies adorning the lid.

Father Nick offered his hand to each person before opening his Bible. "My friends, we mourn the passing of this dear little one into the Great Beyond. In our sorrow, we are called to bow to the will of the all-wise Providence. Let us pray."

The service lasted about fifteen minutes. Afterward, Evan picked up the casket and solemnly placed it in the ground. Everyone took a handful of dirt and dropped it on the casket, except Margaret, who wept into her handkerchief. After his contribution, Robert hobbled back to the Ford, brushing angrily at the clinging soil. As he leaned against the door, he noticed Father Nick glancing his way. Robert crossed his arms defiantly.

Evan turned to the city worker who'd begun to fill in the grave. "The stone angel has been ordered from Sears and Roebuck, but it won't be delivered until next week," Evan explained. The worker nodded. "You'll see it gets placed properly?"

Another nod. It didn't take long for the worker to accomplish his task. He tapped the dirt into a mound, and then walked toward his truck, shouldering the shovel.

Mr. Callahan joined the group and began to lead them to the queue of automobiles.

"Wait," Margaret stopped her mother's pushing. Struggling to get out of the wheelchair, Margaret refused help. She slowly kneeled by the grave and patted the mound smooth. Taking the calla lilies, she carefully placed each one in an array on top. "There," she sniffed. "All tucked in."

Evan tenderly lifted and settled her in the wheelchair again. "You're a good mother, Margaret." He indicated he would push his wife to the waiting automobile.

Mr. Callahan drove the hearse back to town while the mourners followed. Along the route, foot and automobile traffic halted, out of respect.

Grace's Mary Janes barely skimmed the blades of grass as her swing swooshed swiftly past the ground beneath her. The thick tree limb it was attached to croaked in rhythm.

"Slow down there!" Oak said, his voice tinged with worry.

"Have you ever thought about dying?" Grace called. Her braids flew perpendicular behind her.

Oak sat on the back step, reading the paper. At his feet, Grace's jump rope lay scrambled where she'd dropped it moments before. He stood up, ready to catch his sister if she fell. "Unlike you, I rarely think of such things. You're exceptionally, er, somber, Grace."

Her face crinkled at Oak's criticism. "Behold, Thou hast made my days as an handbreadth and mine age is as nothing before Thee." Her words disappeared into the air, the higher she went.

"Huh?"

"The priest quoted that today. At the funeral."

Oak was ashamed he hadn't remembered the funeral until he saw his father's shop closed and the black sash across the door. His deliveries would have prevented him from attending, but he should have remembered. "Why don't you wait until you're old before thinking about dying?"

"Young people, even babies, die."

Oak couldn't argue. "Do you remember when you had scarlet fever and had to stay at Aunt Blossom's under quarantine?"

Grace dragged her feet until she stopped. "Yes. I remember looking out Auntie's living room window and waving to Mother, who stood on the sidewalk. Just then, an automobile pulled up to the house and the driver got out. He'd carried a notice that Auntie told me said "Scarlet Fever" in bright red letters. After attaching it to the front door, he left, and so did Mother. It was a long, lonely time."

"You were seven, right? And a pretty happy kid. Ever since then, you've had this dark fixation about death."

"Sometimes I wish I'd hurry up and die and get it over with. I get tired of worrying what's going to kill me or my family."

Thunder rumbled overhead. Oak hadn't noticed the clouds coming in. Maybe Grace was right, and summer *was* never going to come. He waved his sister over to his side. "No one dies before his appointed time, Grace. So why don't you try not worrying?"

"How?"

"Well," Oak was momentarily stumped. "Ah, how about this? When you start to worry, go for a walk on stilts, or play with your clothespin dollies, or catch a frog and scare Mother. Be a kid." Grace giggled.

Oak felt a drop of moisture on his nose. Holding his hand out, he tried to catch another drop. "When was the last time you jumped in a rain puddle?"

Grace wrapped her arms around Oak and hugged him. "Maybe I'll give it a try."

"Attagirl!"

"Oak, you're my favorite brother."

"I'm your *only* brother."

"That's beside the point."

Oak ruffled her bangs. "Enjoy your childhood, sis, because when childhood's over, life really gets complicated."

"What do you mean?" Grace tucked her arm through Oak's and leaned her head on his shoulder.

"Never mind." He pulled her arm out and stood up. "Need to go. Have a man named Slim Jim to see. Do you know where the umbrella is?"

⟡

Later, Grace came into the kitchen, dripping wet. Her mother, who was fixing supper, looked askance. "My land, what have you been doing, young lady?"

Grace sloshed out of the room, calling over her shoulder, "It's all Oak's fault, Mother. Talk to him." She skipped all the way to her bedroom.

⟡

After supper, Eulila asked Robert to make a fire in the fireplace. "I can't believe we have to do this in June!"

Her gaze followed her husband as he went through the routine of building a fire. He had barely said twenty words since the funeral. When the crunched newspapers ignited, Robert used the bellows. Soon they sat in companionable silence and watched the dancing flames.

"Would you like some hot chocolate?"

Robert nodded.

While Eulila was heating the chocolate pieces in the double boiler, someone knocked on the door.

"Can you get that, dear?"

She heard a man's voice, then Robert's. They became muffled as the two moved into the living room. Removing the double boiler from heat, Eulila went to see who'd arrived.

"Why, hello, Father Nick. What brings you here?"

"I was strolling by and saw the smoke. I couldn't resist." Robert had taken the priest's jacket and hung it on the hall tree.

"You were walking in this weather?" She led him to her own chair.

"I like interacting with the elements. It makes me feel closer to God."

"Would you like some hot chocolate? I was fixing some for us."

Father Nick rubbed his hands together. "That would be delightful, my dear woman."

Robert waited until she'd left the room. "Did Evan send you, Father?"

"And why should he do that?"

"He's concerned about me, I know."

"Oh?"

The room became silent but for the occasional pop from the fireplace. After a while, Father Nick got up and took the tongs. With care, he separated a burning ember from its nest and placed it to one side of the hearth. Then he sat down again. Both men watched as the ember's brightness dimmed into gray ash. A few more minutes passed and Father Nick got up again. This time he moved the cold, dead ember to the middle of the fire. It began to glow immediately. He sat down. Robert glanced at the priest, then at the fire.

"I added some cinnamon to the chocolate and whipped some cream to crown it. I hope you didn't mind waiting."

Eulila carried in a tray with three mugs balanced on it. She handed the men theirs, then stood near the fireplace to warm up.

Father Nick wrapped his hands around the steaming cup. "Not at all. We've had a most interesting conversation."

Robert squinted at the fire. "Indeed, the good Father has quite a way with words."

"Mm, this is delicious, Mrs. Miller."

"Call me Eulila."

❧❧

Later, as Robert walked Father Nick to the door, he said, "It's been too long since I've seen the inside of a church."

"Then it's about time you reacquainted yourself."

Robert rubbed his chin. "Maybe it is. Good night, then."

Father Nick opened the door. "Ah, the rain has finally stopped. Farewell, Robert."

Chapter Eight

"Mr. Miller, that is ingenious! Ah knew you were to be trusted." It was Thursday and Evan had just returned with the Jones family.

Robert rolled up the drawing of a bicycle and set aside the paper doll he'd made, representing Susie. On a 1:6 scale, he'd used pushpins for knees, elbows, ankles, and neck joints. Placing the paper doll on the drawing, he'd mimicked motions similar to Susie pedaling. From that he had adjusted the real bicycle to accommodate the little girl's handicap.

"Come heah, Susie, and try it out." John Jones used a hand to scuttle his youngest to her bicycle and steadied it as she hopped on. Robert held on to the seat and pushed her out the back door to the alley. The Jones family followed and cheered her on as she got the hang of riding. Susie's face showed fear, then concentration, and then finally elation.

When Jones attempted to pay, Robert held up his hand. "Buy your family a celebration meal at the LaCourt."

"That's mawty fine of you, Mr. Miller. May God bless you."

As the Jones family pushed Susie's bicycle through the entrance, Robert wondered if he'd see them again. Every member now had a bicycle. Given their proclivity for sticking together, he was surprised they'd never asked for a tandem. Of course, if they had, he'd have sent them down to Porter Carson's shop. Tandems were his expertise.

Percival Harrison elbowed his way into the shop, the bell jangling angrily. "That door nearly broke my new cane, Miller! Is that how good customers are treated? Percival raised a curly wooden cane above his head. I just purchased it, and if there's one scratch, why I'll —"

"Evan, how is Mr. Harrison's transportation coming?"

"Once again, my admiration." Dalton slapped a newspaper on the desk. "You may yet be a worthy replacement." Oak gasped when he saw the front page and his byline under the headline:

Better Homes Means Greater Happiness

"This is a surprise!"

"Let's take a walk."

The weather had finally started to act like summer. Flies buzzed in and out of foot traffic while birds twittered from one perch to another, tending lofty nests above Main Street storefronts. Humidity and heat attacked the morning like a swarm of mosquitoes, sapping everyone's strength.

Oak mopped his forehead. "Sometimes I forget we live in a desert."

Dalton agreed. "Mind if I say hello to my father?" The two men poked their heads in Bert Benge's store. It was at least five degrees cooler there. Situated on several shelves, metal fans frenzied the air. Each had a bowl of chipped ice in front, cooling the flow passing over it. Orus Trumbo waved to his son, indicating he'd be with him in a moment. He opened a box of dress shoes for his customer, an officious gentleman with a patronizing posture. The image was reinforced by his waxed handlebar mustache and wire glasses pinched on the tip of his aquiline nose.

"Walk-Over sole leather will out-walk any sole leather at any price." Orus turned the shoe over. "The pear-shaped heel has made this the largest selling shoe on the market. Shall we try it on?"

The man scrutinized the shoe, folding it nearly in half, sniffing the leather, picking at the stitches. He nodded to Orus, who used a shoehorn to slip each shoe on. Standing up, the customer stomped around, harrumphing at each step.

Orus Trumbo excused himself and came over to the young men. He carried himself with elegance, his intelligent eyes serene; his bushy mustache and dark brown hair were combed fastidiously, and his immaculate clothes fitted him exceptionally well. But oddly, dirt outlined his fingernails. "He'll be at that for a few moments. You'd think he was purchasing an automobile instead of a pair of Sunday-go-to-meeting shoes. Still I'll keep my peace."

"Never miss a good chance to shut up."

At the same time father and son finished the saying. Both grinned.

"Will Rogers?" asked Oak.

"Good guess," replied Dalton.

Orus held out his hand, and Oak introduced himself.

"Call me O.B."

"I think your customer is needing attention, O.B.," observed Dalton.

Orus's mustache quivered. "Dalton, you can call me 'Father.' Back to earning my dime. Thanks for stopping by. Nice to meet you, Oak." Orus Trumbo glided back to his customer.

The young men collided with the humidity as they returned to the street. A few doors down, they gladly entered Mesa Drug.

"You and your father seem to have a good relationship," commented Oak.

"Depends on his mood. You know what they say about Colorado weather? If it's sunny, just wait a minute and it will be pouring. That about sums up our relationship."

"Oh?"

"Some days, his cool air meets my warm, and lightning strikes. I try and avoid all the bad weather I can with him. For instance, he'd be mighty mad if he knew I'd gone with Walter Walker to Delta to attend the Methodist minister's funeral."

"Why?" Oak took the vanilla-caramel malted from the waitress. Setting it down, he dipped his spoon in the whipped cream and stuck it in his mouth.

"Because the Ku Klux Klan made an appearance."

Oak raised an eyebrow. "What did they do?"

"They laid a flowered cross on the casket." He drew closer to Oak and whispered, "It was eerie. They didn't say a word."

"What does a flowered cross mean?"

"Walker said it meant they approved of the man."

"Flowered crosses for those they approve of, and burning crosses for those they don't," Oak said derisively. "Sounds sinister, but I don't know much about secret organizations."

"Aw, they're harmless." Dalton sipped his cola through a straw. "But try convincing my father of that. He hates the KKK. He wouldn't even let me see *Birth of a Nation* when it played at the Avalon." He grinned. "I get my stubbornness from him, so I asked Father for the $19 to purchase a KKK uniform. He said I could join the KKK or go to college." Dalton shrugged. "He won that round. I chose college."

"Your father seems an intelligent man." Oak scraped the bottom of the glass to get the last of the caramel.

"Not everyone appreciates my father. He's a dreamer. He doesn't 'fit' the mold, he 'creates' it."

"My father still lives in the trenches," Oak muttered.

"Let's talk about you, Oak. Tell me what article you enjoyed writing the most."

Oak thought about it. He'd had an assignment every day this week.

It had been rewarding to interview the train conductor who'd seen Roy Johnson flailing in the Gunnison River shortly after noon on the day he disappeared. Though the body hadn't been found yet, at least the matter of his death seemed settled.

The boxing match at the Armory Wednesday night was exciting. Reporting the ten-round bout between Luther "Watt" McCarthy and Ed Faber truly was a "Cracken Good Battle Royal," as it was promoted. He especially enjoyed the energy of the audience that responded enthusiastically to the fight. Everyone seemed to have had fun, even the battered boxers.

Better Homes and Gardens Week activities helped Oak, and hopefully his readers, understand how progressive Grand Junction really was. His pride was well placed within his words.

"I can't choose. They all were interesting to write about. Why do you ask?"

"Here's what I see." Dalton pulled out his pad and pencil. After touching the tip of the pencil to his tongue, he wrote a flamboyant "1" in the upper corner of a blank page. "There is no doubt you have talent." He wrote "talent."

"Number two — you have drive, ambition. Number three — you have a strong work ethic. Number four — you care about what you are writing about. Number five — you want to make a difference."

"Sounds like the makings of a successful New York reporter to me." Oak pretended to flutter a cigar in his mouth.

"And number six — he doesn't know it yet, but he's the perfect *hometown* reporter." Dalton sat back and waited for that to register.

"Beg pardon?" Oak had stopped mid-flutter.

Dalton cocked an amused eyebrow. "You've said you want to teach about great social issues; to benefit the masses. To make a difference."

Oak nodded vigorously. "Yes . . . "

Dalton held up the piece of paper. "You made a big difference this week. You crafted the soul of this thriving town into meaningful words and phrases. You informed, encouraged, comforted, and praised it. You have a unique gift, Oak, and I think it would be wasted in the big city. You belong here."

"You're wrong!" Oak stood up so fast his chair fell backwards. "I want to go to New York. It's my dream!"

"Listen to me —"

Oak shook his head. "I've got to go." He threw a coin on the table and stormed out.

The Majestic's motto, "The Theatre That Delivers The Goods," was gold embossed across the top of the ticket booth window. The glass-enclosed booth was centered beneath the arched façade, a wide entryway behind it. A line of patrons, in quiet conversation, meandered down the sidewalk. Posters decorated the outside walls; the left side presenting the current movie, the right side announcing what was appearing next.

"That looks interesting."

Oak, Lazuli, and Fluff turned as a man behind them pointed. A triple program was planned for the weekend: Gloria Swanson in *Prodigal Daughters,* and two comedies, *An Eastern Westerner* with Harold Lloyd, and *Felix Minds the Kids* with comic, Pat Sullivan.

"We should make a date for that," Lazuli murmured. "Alone." They were waiting to see *Sherlock, Jr.* starring Buster Keaton and Kathryn McGuire.

"I hear Buster plays a film projectionist who has dreams of becoming a detective," Oak said, pointing to the poster of a deadpan Buster Keaton leaning against a ticket booth manned by pretty Kathryn McGuire.

"Typical. Hollywood is always trying to elevate the common man." Fluff yawned. "People should accept the fact that some are meant for greatness and some are meant for, well, not."

Oak squinted at Fluff. *Is she talking about people like me? Or her?*

"I disagree. I think everyone should try to rise above their circumstances and become their best. Isn't that what Better Homes and Gardens Week was all about, Oak?" Lazuli slipped an arm through Oak's.

"Hadn't thought of it that way, but yes."

Fluff nudged her shoulder between the couple, separating them. "I'm bored with this subject. Say, are we going to sit in the" she laid her cheek against her folded hands and cooed "balcony?"

Fluff trying to be romantic was scary. Oak turned away and handed a couple of coins to the ticket girl. "He's paying for mine, too." Fluff batted her eyelashes at Oak. Resigned, he dropped another dime on the counter. He didn't know how she'd managed it, but Fluff had tagged along for the meal at Your Cafeteria and now, the movie. He'd have to get an extra job if this happened every time he took Lazuli out.

He couldn't take his eyes off of Lazuli. She was radiant in a silvery dress, with dropped waist, pin tucking, and handkerchief hem. Tonight, instead of a hat, she wore a beaded headband. It twinkled under the lighted marquee.

She was attentive to him, too. Every time Oak looked at her, her blue gaze was already meeting his.

He switched places with Fluff and took Lazuli's arm. The next instant he was catching her before she fell to the floor. "Fluff, I'm warning you!"

"What's eating you?" The girl's face was belligerent.

"Oak, that was me — this time. These new shoes have the highest heels." She reached down and pulled them off. "What we girls do for you men! Come on!" She padded into the carpeted lobby, pulling Oak with her. "I can hear the music already."

It was decided to sit in the balcony after all. That area was usually full of "spooners," which didn't bother Oak in the least. To be seen going to the balcony with the most beautiful girl in town would do wonders for his ego, not to mention his reputation.

He trailed Lazuli up the stairs, checking his image in the mirror on the wall. He straightened his tie.

"Don't you know that short ties are passé?" Fluff tsk-tsked. Shaking her head, she filed by Oak and caught up to Lazuli.

Damn! Oak buttoned his vest.

"Let's sit in the very back, Lazy."

"Then we can't see the movie very well."

"Who wants to watch the movie?"

"Believe it or not, we do."

"Fine! I get to sit in McClintock's chair."

Fluff stomped over several pairs of feet before she reached the wide chair made just for Merle McClintock, a large-framed correspondent for the *Sentinel*. It spanned the width of two normal seats. A duplicate version was at the Avalon Theater. Fluff plumped down in it with a huge sigh.

"I hope Merle isn't attending the movie tonight," whispered Oak. "She'll have a fight on her hands." Lazuli feigned dismay.

The couple settled next to Fluff, and Lazuli immediately placed Oak's arm around her shoulders. She snuggled closer and laid her temple against his cheek.

At that moment, the pianist stopped her prelude and began the movie's accompaniment. Only the Avalon had a full-fledged orchestra to play a movie's musical score, but the pianist at the Majestic was exceptionally talented.

The velvet curtains opened and Buster Keaton, wearing his trademark porkpie hat, appeared. The movie house broke out in cheers. As the story commenced, a continual retinue of laughter, booing, sighs, and gasps ensued. The piano added drama, sadness, silliness, and romance to the narrative on screen.

The story was about a man who is falsely accused of stealing the watch of his girlfriend's father. He falls asleep in a theatre and dreams he becomes part of the detective movie on screen. As Sherlock, Jr., Buster Keaton's character solves the crime, but not without many pratfalls and missteps. It was so funny, Oak forgot to neck with his date.

"I knew it was his rival that stole the watch!" Lazuli said, as the threesome stood on the sidewalk outside the Majestic and discussed the plot.

"I thought the father had simply lost it, and just couldn't admit it." Fluff looked like she had actually enjoyed herself. Her smile transformed her face.

It's amazing how a cheery attitude changes one's countenance. Oak felt so affable, he offered to drive Fluff home. "We'll go up to Orchard Mesa first," he quickly said, so there was no misunderstanding. He wanted the rest of the evening alone with Lazuli.

After Fluff was dropped off, the couple motored into town. They took the long way, past old Palmer Park, which now was part of the cemetery.

"Cemeteries scare me." Lazuli scooted close to Oak. Oak felt her shiver and cursed cemeteries and anything else that would attack the sensibilities of the sweet young woman on his arm.

It was still early, ten o'clock, so they decided to drive to Lover's Lane, near Second Fruit Ridge. The Ford joined a long row of vehicles parked in the dark.

Lazuli slipped out of her shoes, crossed her legs and leaned against Oak. A glimpse of silk stockings, rolled below her knees set Oak's heart to whacking his ribs. Now that he had Lazuli where he'd never thought she'd be, he wasn't sure what to do. His lips suddenly felt like alligator hide.

"Have I ever told you I wanted to be an actress?" Lazuli asked, a bit breathy. She sounded as nervous as Oak felt. He relaxed a little.

"Wanted?"

"That was after I'd decided I didn't want to be a politician and before I wanted to be a veterinarian."

"Can a girl be a veterinarian?"

Lazuli sat up. "Of course, silly. Women have been all sorts of things, even doctors. It just hasn't been advertised."

Oak's mouth formed an 'O' in the dark. He hoped he hadn't offended Lazuli.

"Men have it so easy. They can be anything they want. I can't wait for the day when a girl can say, 'I want to be a veterinarian,' and her boyfriend doesn't gulp."

Boyfriend? "You mean you don't want to become a 'stenog' and marry your boss, like every other modern woman?"

"I have different plans for marriage, thank you very much."

"Well, if I wanted to get married, I'd definitely consider going into business for myself. As the boss, I could have my pick!" Oak laughed.

"You're teasing! What a wretched man you are," Lazuli pouted, then wrinkled her nose to show she was kidding.

"Back to the subject at hand, Miss. Men don't have it all that easy. Sure they can make choices, but there's always someone to say you aren't good enough, or that's not the right job for you, or you're not smart or good-looking enough." Oak ended on a sour note.

Lazuli twisted her body so she was facing Oak. "Oh, my! Has that happened to you?"

Yowzah! Her eyes are dazzling when she looks at me like that!

"M-maybe." He pulled at his collar. *To hell with it!* He whipped his tie off.

Lazuli put her mouth next to his ear. "Well," she murmured, "they were lying."

"You don't say." Hungrily, he met her lips.

They pulled apart at the same time. Lazuli opened her door and stepped into the cool breeze. She wrapped her arms around herself. Oak joined her. "I hope I didn't overstep my — "

She put her fingers on his mouth. "As you are so fond of saying, it was my pleasure. Too much pleasure, I might add. I want you to know I'm not the fresh type. This is my, um, first petting party."

"You don't say?" *Her first?*

Lazuli put her fingers beneath Oak's chin and snapped his mouth shut. "In spite of this," she pulled at her flapper dress, "I'm really an old-fashioned girl."

Oak was relieved. "That makes two of us."

"You're an old-fashioned girl, too?" Lazuli threw her head back, laughing. "I've always wanted a sister."

"Silly girl."

Parked in front of her house, Lazuli seemed reluctant to go in. Oak wanted the night to go on, but . . .

"One minute until curfew. We don't want to upset your parents. Or mine."

"They're wrong, you know."

"Who? Our parents?"

"Whoever said you weren't good enough, smart enough, or handsome enough."

"Oh."

"Anyone can see you're a man of dimension, endowed with maturity, good judgment, and — and kind eyes!"

In other words, I'm plain as pudding, but at least I'm nutritious. Amused, Oak chewed on the inside of his cheek. "Glad you think so highly of me."

"I'm all balled up here!" Lazuli grabbed his hand. "What I'm trying to say is you shouldn't shortchange yourself."

"It isn't me doing the shortchanging. I have the smarts, I have the drive, and I have the talent. Yet, no one seems to think I can follow my dream. Maybe if I looked like Valentino — "

"He *is* the cat's meow!"

"Exactly. Wealthy, successful, talented, the star of every girl's dream, and I bet it was his looks that opened the door."

"There's more than one way to open a door! Look at, um, Buster Keaton!" Lazuli was triumphant. *She has a point.* "Beauty isn't everything."

"And the lovely Lazuli knows this personally."

"You think beauty makes my life better?" she scoffed. "It only complicates it."

"Is that so?" Oak's tone challenged her.

"May I remind you of Fluff and Dugger?" The Ford filled with amiable laughter. When it had settled down, Lazuli pulled on Oak's earlobe. "I like being with you, Oak. You have my best interests in mind." She nuzzled his cheek. "I feel comfortable and safe."

Hope she doesn't mean that in a worn-out-bedroom-slipper kind of comfortable and safe!

Her goodnight kiss said otherwise.

❦

"Robert?"

"Mmm?"

"Remember when we were young?"

Robert chuckled. "A lifetime ago?"

"We had so much fun!"

Robert looked down at his wooden peg. The last time he'd had "fun" was before the war.

Robert and Eulila sat together on the porch swing. The strawberry moon rising in the south sky cast a faint glow on the street scene. The couple rocked in silence while crickets serenaded from the liquid shadows.

"We used to dance every Friday night."

"In your uncle's living room."

"With his dilapidated Victrola."

"Those were the good old days, Lila."

"I miss dancing. With your strong arms around my waist, I felt like nothing bad could touch me as long as you were near." Eulila slipped her hand through the crook of her husband's arm. "Together we seemed invincible." She laughed lightly. "Foolish, aren't I?"

Was she? Robert looked down on his wife. Laugh lines had just begun etching their way into her smooth skin. That amazed him. He'd given her no reason for mirth these six long years, yet she'd kept her sense of humor. That was probably the reason they were still married. He reached over and caressed her cheek. She pushed against his hand with her lips and kissed his palm.

Robert felt something stir deep within his soul, a tiny sprig of hope breaking through the crusty wilderness of his heart. Before he knew it, he was standing in front of his wife. He bowed, and then held out his arms.

"Why, Robert. Are you sure?"

He folded her close and as they waltzed on the porch, his soft humming turned to song.

> *Roses are shining in Picardy*
> *In the hush of the silver dew;*
> *Roses are flowering in Picardy*
> *But there's never a rose like you . . .*

Eulila's soprano joined her husband's graveled voice.

> *And the roses will die with the summer time*
> *And our roads may be far apart;*
> *But there's one rose that dies not in Picardy*
> *'Tis the rose that I keep in my heart.*

Robert lifted his wife's chin and kissed her for a long time.

The sweet midnight air enveloped the renewed lovers, whirling past them and through the screened door, where it rustled the curtain that Grace stood behind. With a satisfied nod, she carried her glass of water back to her bedroom.

Chapter Nine

"Mother, may I speak to you?" Oak had barely slept the night before, and he needed to talk to someone about Lazuli.

"Oh, Oak! I'm so glad you came by. Mr. Moyer is up in his office and would like to see you." Eulila's cheeks were flushed pink and her eyes sparkled unnaturally.

"Am I in trouble?"

Eulila laughed. "On the contrary, you will be most pleased. Run along, dear. Don't keep the man waiting."

Oak climbed the stairs to the first floor mezzanine, wondering what his mother was so excited about. He'd been introduced to "Uncle Billy" many years before. If his memory served him right, the first time was on the occasion of him using Grace's tea set to excavate the "ruins" he'd found in the neighbor's chicken coop.

"Thank you, William, for your timely advice. Please use those funds accordingly, but keep out one percent to help the Cooper family, would you?"

A woman stood in the doorway of William Moyer's office, her back to Oak. He waited on the top step for her to finish her business and pass him. Mrs. Ullery, who sat at a desk overlooking the first floor, had a displeased set to her face. She furiously rearranged piles of receipts, snapping each stack on the table before moving on to the next. *What's the matter with the woman?*

Oak was astounded when the visitor turned around. It was Nell Page. Of 538 South Avenue fame. The Row. *Interesting! What is she doing at the Fair?* Oak had never been this close to a madam. His fingers itched for his notepad.

Broken Jaw Nell, her age indeterminate, leaned upon a mannish umbrella, which complemented her orange shift, patterned with hunting motif. An angled hat accented in sweeping pheasant tail feathers adorned her bobbed brown hair. Though not considered pretty, Nell's face was far from unpleasant. Creamy skin and fine bone structure defied age. Her eyes, straightforward and hooded by droopy lids, gave the impression of petulance, but her misshapen mouth confirmed it. A large bowtie partially camouflaged that awkward feature.

Oak wondered if she was nicknamed "Broken Jaw" Nell because of a birth defect or because of some legendary fight in a tavern. Oak recollected Dalton's question at the banquet about names. If ever a moniker could change the course of a life . . .

"Good afternoon, young man." Nell's gaze was direct and unabashed.

"Ma'am." Oak touched his brow politely.

Sniff! "How nice to be treated like a lady." She threw a critical eye in Mrs. Ullery's direction. Snap! from the desk. Heavy perfume followed Nell Page down the stairs.

Oak wished he had time to delve deeper into the scenario. There might be a great story here. He took note of Mrs. Ullery's indignant face and decided it was not the time for an interview.

"I'm here to see Mr. Moyer," Oak answered the accountant's terse inquiry.

"Oak, my boy! Come in and sit down." Mr. Moyer walked to the door and closed it behind Oak. He turned with a deprecating cough. "Do you have any idea why you are here?" He indicated that Oak should sit.

"Not a clue, sir." The woven chair seat still felt warm. Nell Page's perfume cloyed the air.

"Well," delight dripped from Moyer's voice. He adjusted his carnation as he moved around his small wooden desk, his chair creaking when he sat down. The elderly man folded his hands on the clean desktop. He beamed at Oak.

The window was open behind him, a potted fern balanced on the sill. Below, Oak could hear the din of traffic. A ceiling fan whirred overhead and a fly landed on his hand. He swatted at it.

"Um, sir?"

"Yes, ahem. What I'm about to say, I'd like not to leave this room."

Oak leaned forward, instantly at attention.

"I heard you have plans to go to the big city and make a name for yourself. Now don't look so startled, young Miller. Word gets around.

"I've read with interest your articles in the *Sentinel* this week. Excellent! You and I have the same pride and vision for our little town. I can't help but believe you could, indeed, make a name for yourself.

"Finances have been sparse at your father's business, yet I hear he sometimes refuses payment from the poorer families. I admire that." This was news to Oak.

Mr. Moyer opened a drawer and placed a single sheet of paper on his desk. "A fine mind like yours should be heading off to college this fall, yet with no funds . . . " He pushed the paper close enough to Oak that he could read it. The letter-head announced University of Colorado. "It would be my privilege to pay for your college education. I know this is a grave thing to consider, but time is short. You have less than a month to decide."

"Mother? I need to talk with you!" Oak whispered loudly. Eulila flapped her hand to say it would be a minute. Her attention returned to a stoop-shouldered girl in a drab cloth dress standing next to her.

"She's breaking in the new girl." Lillian Gesberg appeared at Oak's elbow. "Sometimes I wonder where Stoneface, er, Mrs. Stone finds them. This one looks like a war waif. She's probably a stray that Dad Smith found by the train tracks, on his deliveries. That happens a lot, you know. I hope they gave her an intelligence test, like I had."

Oak observed the new girl. "Looks can be deceiving, don't you think?"

"Oh, I am sorry. How awfully insensitive I can be. I'm rather preoccupied. Some days it's about health, some days I wonder what her personality will be like. Today, it's appearance. I hope she doesn't inherit this." Lillian parted her lips to frame the gap between her teeth. Oak wondered if the woman had gone mad.

Lillian tittered. "You have no idea what I'm talking about, do you?" Oak shook his head. "Our little darling." She patted her middle. "She's due in November, but I think about her all the time."

Ah. "It's a rather endearing attribute, that gap."

This entertained Lillian. "Endearing, eh? I never thought of it that way. Ah-choo! Bless me, I can't seem to get over this cold. Such a sore throat I have." She withdrew a lacy handkerchief and sniffed into it.

"Place a crushed spider way back in your mouth. That should take care of it."

Lillian blinked. "Yes, well, I doubt I'll ever complain of a sore throat again. Say, it looks like your mother is finishing up. I'm off to break. Need to find some peanut butter!"

"Now don't let Mrs. Stone frighten you," imparted Eulila to the trembling girl. "She's really harmless. If you'll take that aisle, you'll find her desk. When you've finished with the forms, she'll send you down the street to Dr. Munro, the health inspector. After his examination, you'll report back to the office. The process will be over before you know it, and then we can begin training!"

If not a war waif, the girl looked shell-shocked to Oak.

"Th-th-thank you, Mrs. Miller."

"Oh dear," Eulila said to her son after the girl departed, "we'll have to work that out. Do you think she's just scared or really has a stutter?"

"You'll find a way to make it work, I'm sure. Mother, did you know what Mr. Moyer was going to do?"

"It was a surprise to your father and I. He told us this morning." She put her arm around Oak's shoulders and directed him away from the other clerks. "It's got to remain anonymous to the rest of the world, but naturally the dear man had to tell us. Oak! Your dream is finally going to come true!"

For some reason, Oak wasn't as excited as he thought he should be. "Yes, well, I must do deliveries. See you at supper?"

"Well!" Eulila said as she watched her son wend his way through the aisles to the elevator. The doors closed on his thoughtful face.

Oak went through the motions of delivering newspapers, but he sleepwalked the entire route. He stared stupidly at his empty bag as he stood in front of the *Sentinel* office.

"Girlfriend give you the bum's rush?"

"Huh?"

"You look lost." Dalton Trumbo leaned against a pillar. "Been waiting for you."

Oak folded his bag in half, then half again and stuck it under his arm. This gave him time to decide if he wanted to talk to Dalton. "Why?" he finally asked.

"I need to apologize."

Startled, Oak dropped the bag. He bent to pick it up, but Dalton was there before him.

"Truce?" he said, handing Oak the bag.

"You're quite fond of java, aren't you?"

Oak put his empty cup down on the table. "Well, if you can't drink moonshine. . ."

Dalton laughed, a little too heartily. *Why, the great man is nervous! Imagine that!*

They were sitting in the *Sentinel*'s break room. Dalton took a puff on his cigarette, exhaling the smoke in a billow. "I owe you an apology, Miller. Now that's about as sentimental as I'm going to get. If you want tears, go see your mammy."

"Exactly what are you apologizing for?"

"Maybe I was a little jealous. I see something in your work that I wish I had — that ability to connect on a soul level. I'll have to work on it."

"So, you're apologizing for being jealous?"

"Well, no. I was, er, wrong to squelch your dream." Dalton slugged Oak's arm. "I'm trying to tell you to reach for the moon! I believe that you, of all people, can do it."

"I'm not sure about anything, anymore." Oak got up and refilled his coffee cup. He saw he'd taken the last cup and proceeded to start another pot. "I've been thinking. Maybe you were right. Perhaps, I'm just meant to stay in this little town."

"An option, but don't stay on my account — "

"An opportunity fell in my lap today. If I take it, I'll be heading to Boulder this fall."

Dalton looked genuinely pleased. "You'll be Joe College, like me! We should room together."

Oak looked thoughtfully at Dalton. He never dreamed he'd even talk to the man, let alone room with him at college. There was so much he could learn . . . So why his hesitation?

"I haven't decided to take it yet. If I go, I'll have to do something," Oak fanned his hands outward from his face and mimed a Hollywood smile, "big with my life, don't you think? Can't let a college education — a free one, especially — go to waste."

"An education never goes to waste, whether it's used in New York or Grand Junction. William Moyer once told me all the great minds grow up and leave this town. Maybe one of those great minds will decide to return this time."

Oak looked steadily at Dalton. "And make a difference?"

Dalton nodded. "It's up to you, my good man. Whatever you decide, think hard on it first. Take other opinions into account, but remember this decision will steer the course of your life, and you want to be satisfied you did the right thing."

"I appreciate those words of wisdom, Dalton." Oak chuckled. "My mother was thrilled at the news. She's my biggest fan."

"I know about doting mothers. My own would do anything to help me achieve my goals." Dalton's face softened. "She's always believed in me. I'll go far because of her. And Father."

"I've never met your mother. What's her name?"

"Maud. Used to be Tillery." He sighed. "She deserves to be serving tea in a grand Victorian on Seventh Street, rather than hard labor in our little shanty. She's tough, though."

"Oh?"

"You might say she had an interesting childhood. She grew up around murderers, thieves, and such."

"Beg pardon?"

Dalton grinned. "Grandfather Tillery was a sheriff for Montrose County. He tracked outlaws with as much tenacity as our own Doc Shores. Once he was on your scent, you might as well throw down your guns and put up your hands.

"He'd bring these miscreants home — the only stop between capture and jail — and house them for the night. After feeding them, he'd give them the run of the place for the night since they all knew it was no use running away. They'd play cards with Mother and her siblings and enjoy the last bit of home cooking they'd eat for years.

"Mother knew her life was different and gleaned what she could from it. But in her heart, she yearned for gentility."

"And then she married your father."

Dalton nodded. "Father was so different from the men she'd been exposed to. He was sensitive. He kept up on current events and the arts, he read books and even discussed them with Mother. He brought gentility to her life but, alas, not riches."

Oak wondered how Maud dealt with Orus's frequent jobs. "Do you think she'll ever get to live in a grand Victorian on Seventh?"

Dalton shook his head. "No, but she's happy. We all are. Mother and Father have lived on their own terms, and they make no apologies. I should be lucky to live as nobly."

One of the regular reporters came in. "Did you hear what happened to Dugger Snyder this morning?"

Oak jumped up. "What?"

"I forgot to tell you." Dalton indicated to the other reporter, who leaned against the counter, he'd give Oak the news.

"That dumbbell was harassing Nell's girls at 538 when the madam stepped in. Obviously he didn't care who he was messing with and Dugger made an off-color remark about her nickname. Nell kindly showed him the exit — headfirst. He hightailed it out of there like his hair was on fire." *I guess that answers the question of her name!* "Dugger hopped in his auto and careened around the corner, crashing that brand new Ford Model T coupe into the back end of a parked vehicle.

"Nell came running and pulled the lad from the wreck. She got him to St. Mary's, but it looks like Dugger may never walk again."

"Then, he'll probably never go to prison for assaulting Margaret Treece and murdering her baby."

Dalton shrugged. "That young man has always been behind bars; he just didn't know it. Arrogance is the worst kind of prison."

Chapter Ten

Oak wandered over to his father's bicycle shop after saying goodbye to Dalton. He leaned against the counter and watched his father, who had just rolled out a three-wheeled bicycle from the workshop. It was low to the ground, had an oversized seat, a large wire basket in back and a smaller one in front. Above the front basket was a lantern. A bulb horn adorned the right handle. Evan stood by his workbench with his hands on his waist as he watched the scene.

"That's perfect!" Percival Harrison shouted as he fidgeted by Robert. Reaching over, he squeezed the horn. It trumpeted loudly. "Whoopee!" Oak had never seen an old man do a jig.

Robert seemed pleased. Oak looked twice at the smile that lighted up his father's face. He couldn't remember the last time he'd seen the phenomenon.

"Well, let's try this flivver out!" cried Percival.

Robert and Evan were amused. Robert guided the bicycle out the back door. Evan held the door open for Harrison. Oak followed at a distance. Robert said, "It will take some getting used to, but, ah, I can see you've already got it figured out. Good man."

Oak watched from the doorway, more interested in his father than Percival's glee. *Why, he makes a difference! People enter this insignificant, grease-stained concrete shop and their lives are changed when they leave.*

After Percival Harrison paid for his purchase, he shook his cane above his head as he shuffled out the back door. There was one last "Whoopee!" that slowly died away.

Evan and Robert shook hands vigorously. "One of your better triumphs, I'd say, Robert."

"We're a team, remember? Nice job, Evan."

Evan acknowledged Oak, and then headed back to his workbench. Robert faced his son.

"Father, I never realized the impact your business has on people."

"Was there something you needed?"

Oak was hurt at his father's formal tone. It had taken courage to offer that olive branch.

Robert bit his lip. "I'm – I'm sorry, Oak. Old habits are hard to break." Robert led his son to his desk and indicated he should sit down. Oak did, on the same chair Margaret had sat on. He waited.

"I've been hard on you, son. Nearly your whole life."

"It hasn't been all bad, Father. Before the war . . . "

"Yes, the war." Robert hung his head. "No excuse for turning a man into a monster. Can you forgive me? I want to do things differently."

Oak didn't know what to say. Forgive his father for not being there for neighborhood plays, Confirmation, or even his high school graduation? Forgive him for humiliating words, being unavailable when a son needed to talk to a father, and for cuffing him in front of Evan? Forgive him for the years Mother pretended everything was all right, and putting the fear of divorce in Grace? That was a high pile to forgive. All these thoughts careened through Oak's mind in moments, and it took even less time to make his decision. He knew there was only one answer to that question.

"Yes, Father. I forgive you."

Robert let out a breath. "Thank you, Oak. I know there is much to forgive, but if you can forgive me, I can," he tapped his knee, "forgive those who did this to me. Us. They really did it to all of us."

"Father, if I may — I know it was terrible losing a leg," Oak turned toward Evan, who was watching intently, "as well as your innocence, and your, er, identity." Robert swiveled to Evan and squinted. Evan shrugged as if saying, "You gotta like the kid's moxie." When Robert swiveled back, Evan nodded at Oak, encouraging him. Oak leaned forward.

"But at one time you were my hero. I'm especially sorry you lost that."

Sunday morning, Oak woke with the dawn in his eyes. He made his cot and wished for the hundredth time he had his own bedroom back. He'd lost it to his sister when she'd reached her second birthday. *Thank you, Grace, for this ten-year-old crick in my neck!*

After delivering papers, he returned just as the household was wakening. Sneaking past Grace's room, he scooted into the bathroom and took a quick bath. His routine took only minutes as he rarely had to shave with his father's straight edge and lather cup. The fine tufts of face hair refused to mature.

He looked at his reflection critically. He'd hoped Lazuli's amorous attentions would magically transform his plain features into something closer to ideal, but the same bland face stared back at him. He stuck his tongue out at it.

"Oak!"

"You bang any harder, Grace, and the door's likely to fall in. I'm not dressed, but I'm sure you'll want a gander at me in my Nainsooks." The clatter ceased. Oak opened the door and peeked out. Steam escaped into the hallway. "I'll be done in two minutes, sis."

"Okey-dokey."

Oak closed the door. He started counting aloud. At "ten" the banging started again. *Right on time.*

"What's that tune you're humming, Mother?" Oak kissed Eulila's cheek as she sliced an apple. "It sounds familiar."

"It's an old favorite, 'By The Light Of The Silvery Moon.' I'm making apple fritters this morning. The *Post* is on the chair." Eulila dropped batter onto her electric skillet. The sunny room filled with fragrant sizzling.

"I haven't heard you hum for a long time." Oak shook the paper open to the funnies. He always read that section first. It helped balance out the bad news that was rampant on the front page, which tended to put him in a bad mood.

"Good morning, Lila."

Oak lowered the paper. His father was standing behind his wife, his hands resting on her shoulders. Eulila raised her cheek to him, and he kissed it soundly.

"Hello, Oak. Ready for church?"

It was then Oak noticed his father was dressed in his Sunday best. "Are you coming with us, Father?" It was hard to keep the wonder out of his voice. *Well, I'll be. Miracles do happen.*

"It seemed a good day to begin." Robert sat down at the table and picked up the front pages.

"Um, Father, you might want to read this section first." He handed him the funnies. *No need to give the devil a head start.*

After Sunday dinner, Oak sat on the front porch step with the paper. He tried to concentrate on the best-written article search, but his mind kept going back to church. Seeing his father sitting next to his mother on the pew made him feel like they were a family again. Pastor Jim's sermon was perfect, as though God Himself had chosen the contents because He knew Robert Miller would be there that morning. The theme was restoration.

"Hello, Oak. Mind if I join you?" Eulila flattened her checkered housedress under her legs and she sat on the stoop.

"Have you noticed Grace hasn't jumped rope once today?" Oak pointed to the rolled up rope in the corner.

"Why do you suppose?"

"Something to do with Father?"

Eulila nodded, her gaze peaceful. "She seems happy. Did you see her at church? Your father's hand had lost all feeling by the time we walked out of there. Even then Grace wouldn't let go!"

"Where is she?"

"She and your father are getting reacquainted over a friendly game of poker."

"Mother!"

Eulila chuckled. "It will take some encouragement to get him to play 'house' with her. In the meantime, don't tell Pastor Jim your father is teaching Grace how to gamble!"

An amiable silence settled on the porch. After a time, Oak said, "I've been thinking about my dream of going to New York." He shifted sideways to better see his mother. "I'm not so sure I want to do that anymore."

Eulila didn't answer right away. Oak saw she was thinking. "Dreams have a mercurial nature, don't you think?" she asked.

"It's certainly turning true for me. You sound experienced."

"Uh-huh," Eulila nodded. "I had a dream once. While growing up in Chicago, my mother and I would visit the grandest of department stores, Marshall Field's, every Saturday. If we didn't have anything to buy, we'd still go, wandering around and watching the cooking classes or fashion shows. A fabulous meal in the restaurant was always a part of the day. Before heading home, Mama and I would slip into one of many elegantly appointed lounges for a cup of tea. We'd mimic the 'ladies' who socialized there." Eulila held up a pretend teacup and elevated her pinky. Her mouth formed a simper. Oak hid his smile.

"I especially loved shopping at Christmas time. The window displays were wintry wonderlands, and when you entered the store you became part of a beautiful postcard. Tinsel, colored bulbs, evergreen boughs, and red ribbons dripped from glass cases and wound around pillars. Carolers sang in each department, and Marshall Field's' Santa had the rosiest cheeks, the biggest belly, and the heartiest laugh in the city."

"A far cry from the Fair Store, eh?"

"For a pioneer town, the Fair has done well. And Dad Smith is a wonderful Santa. Oh! You do know he's played Santa all these years?"

"Mother!"

She grinned. "I'm relieved. I wouldn't want to spoil any childhood fantasies." Eulila drew her knees to her chest and folded her dress around front. "Oak, there was no place like Marshall Field's. I wanted more than anything to work there when I grew up."

"Instead, you wound up in a tiny western town on the fringe of high desert, hitched to a shop owner, saddled with two children, and clerkin' at the Fair." Oak adopted a cowboy twang. "Disappointed?"

Eulila slid her eyes sideways to her son. "Maybe at first, but whenever I felt like complaining, I'd remember the day I met Robert and the decision I made six months later to follow him 'whither thou goest.'" Eulila sighed contentedly. "I have found that God's plans for me are much more satisfying than my own."

"God's plans for you?"

"Uh-huh. 'Man has his dreams, but God directs man's feet.' There's a Bible verse that goes something along that line." Eulila ruffled Oak's hair. "Enough of the sermon. I have other things to talk to you about, son. Tell me about Lazuli."

What could he tell her about Lazuli? That she was the most beautiful woman alive, but also the most levelheaded? That when she looked at him she saw beyond his plainness to his heart? That he'd rather die than see her hurt? "Mother, you're going to call me foolish, but I think I love her."

"Isn't this rather quick?"

"If you call four years 'quick.' I've known from the moment I first saw her that she was the girl for me. I just never thought she'd reciprocate."

"You sound amazed, Oak. You're a fine young man and any girl would be blessed to know you."

"Having my mother think so highly of me doesn't change the fact that, until recently, I'd never had a date," he said. "Yet now the girl of my dreams cares for me. Maybe even loves me."

Eulila shrugged. "There's only one right girl for you, Oak. So what's your next step?"

"I'm not sure. Last week, I had dreams and no way of obtaining them, and now I've got romance and an education in the works and I'm a little scared. What if I fail at both? What should I do, Mother?"

"I don't know, dear. Why not ask your feet?"

"I have to let Mr. Moyer know by tomorrow. "

"What are you going to do, Oak?" Lazuli slipped her hand through the crook of Oak's arm. A surprisingly solid arm to lean on, she thought, but she'd found there were many surprising aspects to Oak. And the more she got to know him, the more her heart longed for him. He wasn't anything like the man she thought she'd marry — and she would marry Oak, make no mistake — yet he was everything she could want in a man. Even her parents approved of him, though they had no idea she was entertaining marriage. Regarding parents, some things were on a need-to-know basis, and she'd let them know after she'd broken the news to Oak. She snuggled closer.

The couple wandered down the network of concrete sidewalks at Lincoln Park, passing the racetrack and stables, the grandstand and bleachers, and the new exhibition hall. Southeast of Moyer Natatorium, the Auto Touring Camp was dotted with vehicles and tents. The air was rife with composting manure from the stables and the nearby zoo that housed Leo, the lion. Oak and Lazuli stopped and sat on the steps in front of the pool to watch the evening tide of people.

"There's a lot to consider in my decision. Dalton said I should think very hard on it so I won't regret it later. But, there are so many things to take into consideration." Oak took Lazuli's hand.

"First, there is you. We've only known each other a short time, Laz. I can't presume I mean anything significant to you, and even if I did, I couldn't expect you to wait for me to finish college. You have your own education to consider."

"I'll meet you for dinner every day."

"Beg pardon?" Oak hopped up and stared down.

"I've been waiting to tell you." Lazuli rose languidly. Putting her hands behind her back, she swiveled her shoulders back and forth. "I'm attending the same university as you. Pre-med. Daddy's going to let me be a veterinarian!"

Oak was careful not to gulp. "That's great news, but," he sat down again, "what if I say no to Moyer?"

Lazuli lighted next to him. "I won't let you! You have a dream to make happen, Mr. Big City Reporter. And-and I want to help you." Lazuli hesitated. "You do want me to help you, don't you?"

"Of course!" Jumping up again, Oak started pacing. He wasn't sure, but he thought Lazuli was implying much more than her words were saying. He had to be careful. He'd learned over the last couple of weeks that women were tricky creatures. Father had been very helpful in that department, but he still felt like a dumbbell when Lazuli was 'chewing gum.'

"Oak Miller, this isn't a sing-along and you aren't a bouncing ball. Please," her voice caressed the word, "sit here." She patted the step next to her.

Gingerly, he sat down.

This brought a wide smile from Lazuli. "You're not very astute, are you? It's a good thing you'll have me around to make sense of it all."

"You don't s – " He didn't get a chance to finish his sentence. His lips became busy.

After a bit of spooning, Lazuli pulled away abruptly. "What about the second?"

Second? Oak moved to kiss her again. She captured his face inches away from hers. "You said 'first' in the list you are taking into consideration. That implies a 'second.'"

It took a moment for Oak to focus on something other than the funny feeling in his stomach, or thereabouts. "I forgot," he murmured.

Lazuli gently pushed Oak away as he reached for her again. "I think that's enough necking for one night. Your eyes are crossing. Seriously, Oak, was there another reason why you wouldn't go to university?"

Oak sighed and collected the strings of sanity that had nearly floated out of reach. "Well, there was the tiniest chance," Oak squeezed his thumb and forefinger together until they were a quarter inch apart, "I'd remain here and work with my father."

"Oh."

"You gulped!"

Far into the night, Oak sat on the porch. Grand Junction slumbered under a blanket of stars, the waning moon half asleep during its watch. He gazed upward, wishing he could see the world from the moon's height instead of from his fool's perspective.

He used to know where he was going and why. Now the clear waters of destiny had been muddied by his blooming love for Lazuli, his father's turnaround, and the unexpected scholarship. Oak was finding it was so much easier *having* a dream, than *living* it.

"Will you be attending the Gesberg's Independence Day picnic tomorrow?" Yum bubbled with her usual enthusiasm. Since school let out, she'd been working every afternoon at the Fair Store. "It'll be the butterfly's boots!"

Eulila finished hanging up the dresses that had been tried on that day. She was exhausted. On her own, she had sold fifteen dresses, three hats, five pair of silk stockings, two purses, and a bathing suit and cap. The other clerks had been just as busy. Business had boomed since summer started.

"Yes, my sweet, we all were invited. Mr. Moyer is even closing the store for the holiday." She touched the delicate cleft in Yum's chin. "Will you be coming with Wilma?"

"And Leonard and little Betty! Do you think there will be, er, boys there?"

"Yum! You're too young to be infatuated with boys. Stick to your dollies, at least until summer's over." *She'll knock them dead when she starts high school.* "Now be a dear and run this tally up to Mrs. Ullery for me."

Eulila watched the winsome girl skip to the elevator. She looked around and seeing no one was looking, she stretched luxuriously, enjoying every crack and pop. Feeling much better she turned toward the dressing room. "Oh! Robert! You startled me. Where'd you come from and what are you doing here?"

Her husband pointed to the stairway behind him. "Today I realized I'd never visited you here." Robert came close and kissed his wife's cheek. "I'm sorry you have to work so hard," he said, with a plaintive look on his face. "You never seem weary at home."

"Nonsense, Robert. I love it here. I get to meet different people, make them feel better about themselves, gossip, and give advice. It's a woman's paradise! No one to feel sorry for here."

"I want to take you away for a vacation, after the summer rush is over."

"Oh, Robert, that would be the, er, butterfly's boots! Where would we go?" She rested her hand on her husband's arm, appreciating its solidness.

"I was thinking of Denver. Evan was telling me about some place called the Brown Palace. He'd read they serve a formal tea every afternoon. You'd like that, wouldn't you?"

"How thoughtful! We must get some new clothes for such a fancy place." Seeing her husband blink at that, she changed the subject. "Oh! Robert, did you happen to see Oak on your way up? He had a meeting with William this afternoon. I'm anxious to see what our son decided."

"I'm afraid not."

"Why don't you wait downstairs while I get my purse? Perhaps he'll wander by. We could give him a ride home." She led Robert toward the stairs, waving goodbye to Mildred Stone, who had arrived to close down the department for the night. Her mouth hung open at the sight of Robert. Eulila kissed her husband full on the lips and heard Mildred gasp.

Yes, Mildred, there is a Mr. Miller and you'll be seeing a lot more of this, I assure you!

Chapter Eleven

"Hurry, Grace, and catch the iceman. We'll need an extra couple of pounds of chipped ice for the watermelon. Here's a clean bucket, payment, and a slice of the fruit bread I made this morning. Be sure and thank Mr. Winters," Eulila called after her daughter.

Grace thought the man couldn't be better named for the profession he was in. She skipped along saying hello to the neighbors, until she caught up with the iceman down the street.

On hot summer days, he was like a flower to bees: children were always swarming around him. Mr. Winters was generous with the little slivers of ice that he chipped off the frozen blocks. Grace loved his grizzled, frizzy comfortableness, but she especially loved the giant workhorses that pulled the ice wagon. Every morning as she lay in bed contemplating getting up, she heard them steadily clopping down the street on deliveries.

"Hello, Jack. Hello, Jill." She gave each one a pat on the nose before finding her place in line.

Shyly, Grace reached out to the children around her, throwing into their conversation a comment here and there. She felt awkward as it had been a long time since she'd had any friends.

"Golly, you're kind of funny!" one pigtailed girl about Grace's age remarked. "I'm Catherine Trumbo. What's your name?" She linked arms with Grace and they chatted until their turns.

The chipped ice seemed to weigh nothing as Grace ran home. Along the way, she counted how many houses had American flags displayed on the street. Ten — a nice round number! The Millers' own wool flag, with its forty-eight stars and thirteen stripes, hung limply from the pole in their front yard, broadcasting that it was going to be a hot holiday, to be sure. Grace stuck a dagger of ice in her mouth and sucked appreciatively.

"Did you remember to say thank you?"

Grace said she did, though she couldn't remember if she had or not. "Mr. Winters stopped his work just to taste your bread, Mother. He said it was the finest he'd sampled in a long time."

"You don't say?" Eulila touched her cheeks. Grace could tell she was pleased. Her mother picked up the bucket of ice and poured it into a wide, shallow metal tub. "Perfect."

Putting her hands on her waist, Eulila surveyed the kitchen. "I think we have everything ready." She pointed as she talked. "The watermelon, of course. Cold meatloaf sandwiches, deviled eggs, celery stalks, green onions, and for dessert, my fruit bread. Oh, yes." Eulila swirled around and removed a pitcher from the icebox. "Lemonade with flowered ice blocks. *Now* we're ready."

Whipping off her apron, she said, "Go get your father and brother. We'll let them load the auto up."

As Grace exited the room, she called over her shoulder, "I made a friend today!"

"I tell you, Robert, I could barely hold back the tears!" The couple was in their bedroom, getting ready to leave for the picnic. Eulila turned around and allowed Robert to clasp her pearl necklace. He brushed his lips against her neck when he was finished.

She leaned against his chest as he wrapped his arms in front of her. Inadvertently, his hand skimmed her breast and she immediately felt a response from him. Her glance was drawn to the made bed. Later, she promised herself.

She cleared her throat. "It seems like everything is going so well. Grace is finally finding friends, Oak is going to college to become a reporter, you — well, I feel like I'm on my honeymoon! Pinch me, Robert." She turned around and nuzzled his smooth cheek. "I want to know this isn't a dream."

"It's a dream come true. Relax, my dear. The hard times are over." He lifted her chin and kissed the tip of her nose. "We better get going before the children miss us. Let's, um, make it an early night, though."

The Ford bumped over the railroad tracks and up the long bridge to Orchard Mesa. The Colorado River ran west in an aquamarine tide. It hadn't rained in at least three weeks; otherwise, the water would be a muddy red with runoff from its tributaries and Grand Mesa. Eulila led her family in song:

> *Daisy, Daisy, give me your answer, do!*
> *I'm half crazy, all for the love of you!*
> *It won't be a stylish marriage,*
> *I can't afford a carriage,*
> *But you'll look sweet upon the seat*
> *Of a bicycle built for two.*

"And Father can build it just for you!" added Grace, in her girlish soprano. Robert and Eulila laughed, but Oak's thoughts had drifted elsewhere.

He hadn't seen Lazuli for two days and his arms ached for her. After a particularly amorous evening, they'd decided that it would be best to refrain from further necking. Oak and Lazuli had discussed their desire to stay celibate, yet it was getting difficult to think straight. He hadn't realized how hard that decision would be and wondered if Lazuli was suffering like he was. It would help being around people. Maybe that was the solution. Just avoid being alone.

The Millers joined other fun-seekers who followed the Midland Trail to the Gesberg farm. After crossing the bridge, the parade of automobiles proceeded to the top of the hill. Turning left, they traversed the main travel route. When the road curved right, they followed it, then turned left with the poles. At the schoolhouse, they jogged to the right, then left, then ahead. They dipped into the wash, thankful it was dry, and curved right close to the river. They passed Four Corners and headed up the hill straight south. Instead of turning east to Whitewater, they wound southwest along a farm road until they came to the Gesberg place.

The electric gate had been rolled back to allow the flow of guests to enter. The Ford trampled over the cattle guard, tagging along after the others, and pulled to a stop in a field near the two-story yellow farmhouse. Small flags on wooden dowels were stuck in the ground hodgepodge, reminding everyone of what the day was all about.

A crowd had already gathered under the trees. Weathered logs lay on the ground, inviting people to sit down and visit. A few had taken advantage of the natural seating, but most families had opened blankets onto the hard ground.

Robert grabbed the watermelon in the tub and asked Oak to bring the heavy picnic basket. Eulila carried the lemonade jug and their checkered blanket, while Grace brought the box with their plates, cups, and utensils. They headed for a stand of young cypress.

"Hello, Eulila. Introduce me and Agnes to your guests." John Gesberg's eyes twinkled as he and his wife approached the Millers.

Agnes Gesberg, dressed in a loose, flowery shift, stood close to her husband. A plain woman with pleasant features, she smiled broadly as Eulila proudly gave the names of her family.

"Welcome to all of you," said John. "Robert, I've heard so many nice things about you over the last few years and now I can place a face with the sentiments. It's mighty good to finally meet you."

John extended his arm to encompass the breadth of his property. "Feel free to wander and mingle. After we've eaten, horseshoes will be that-a-way," he pointed to the barn, "and three-legged races there." He pointed to a woman setting up a table on the grass and folding potato sacks on top. "Later we'll have a sing-along around the fire, followed by fireworks. Leonard Anderegg will be in charge of those."

"Should be a fun evening, all around," Robert said, laying his arm across Eulila's shoulders. He smiled down on her. She saw the warmth in his eyes and the promise in his smile, and squeezed his hand.

"Oh, there's Art and Lillian," said Agnes, looking toward the yellow house. "They've been living with us for the last six months, and with my father here also, it's been crowded. Still I love having family around, especially with a grandbaby on the way! I better go see if they need anything." She bustled off in the direction of the house.

Art had parked his auto in front of the porch and was helping his wife out of the passenger side. Lillian was dressed casually in a pink, sleeveless shirt hanging loosely over sport knickers. Her dark hair had a pink knit cloche stuck on it, and she wore frilly bobby sox with her flats.

Eulila noticed her face was pale with dark circles under her eyes. *Probably overdoing it.*

John chuckled. "My wife's more excited about the little one than I believe Lillian is. Well, if you'll excuse me, I've other guests to meet." With a genial wave, he was gone.

Eulila led her family to the shade and tossed the blanket in the air. She straightened it as it sifted to the ground and pulled the corners square. "Oak, could you lay out the picnic? Oak! Pay attention!"

"Sorry, Mother, I was looking for Lazuli."

"She's over there." Grace pointed to a tight group of people by the elm tree.

"There he goes," Eulila said, throwing a hand up in mock frustration. "Grace would you please set the meal out? Oh, look, there's Evan and Margaret. How nice that she's feeling well enough to celebrate. And I see William Moyer! Robert, let's go say hello."

Grace sighed. Everything was laid out nicely on the blanket, yet no one had returned. She'd rearranged the food alphabetically, then by size. Still no one. Looking around she could see her parents in earnest conversation with Mr. Moyer, and she couldn't see Oak at all. Shrugging, she poured herself a glass of lemonade and reached for a deviled egg, her favorite dish. Too bad if the eggs were all gone by the time her family returned, she thought. They'd had their chance.

"Hello, Grace."

"Catherine! Would you like a deviled egg?"

⚜

"You look delish, Laz."

"And you're a regular Joe Brooks, Oak."

Oak had gone directly to Lazuli. He recognized many of those gathered around her, and greeted them by name. Her friends and coworkers grinned as she excused herself and took Oak's arm. Oak wondered what they thought of him. Lazuli said they were happy for her — all but Fluff, of course, who was never happy.

They wandered across the gully to Harold and Ana Gesberg's house. No one was around, except the curious dog that sniffed their heels as they slipped into the dusky barn. Maybe they should let him follow them. They wouldn't be alone, then, Oak thought. Well, not exactly.

⚜

"What's Fluff s problem, anyway? You realize she hates you?"

"I hope it's not hate. I don't hate her. I feel sorry for her, actually."

The couple sat on a bale of hay in the barn. Shards of misty sunshine sliced through the gaps in the walls while dust and hay sprinkled down from the hayloft like manna. Oak reached up and removed a bit of hay from Lazuli's hair. "Even though she pushes you into dress racks and trips you in front of a crowd?"

"There's something you should know. Fluff is my half-sister. My father was married before."

"Now I've heard everything!"

"My mother's family came from Philadelphia. They were 'new money,' yet highly educated. Of course, her family had never fitted in with the 'old money.'

"And then there was Grandmama and her unpopular ideas. Once she chained herself to the mayor's tree to show how women were imprisoned by society's rules.

"When Mother decided she wanted to teach at university, they moved to Denver, much to the relief of the Easterners. There was plenty of opportunity for her to expand her horizons out west. After all, it was peopled with entrepreneurs and adventurers. Mother could be whom she wanted, and so could Grandmama."

"And Fluff fits in where?"

"Mother was teaching English in Denver when she met Father. He worked as head chef in the cafeteria at the university. She fell instantly in love with his Eggs Benedict, and with him. They married within the year. Soon after I was born, Father revealed he'd been married before, that the woman lived in Grand Junction, and he'd had a child with her.

"The news didn't faze Mother one bit. She insisted they move here and when they were settled, she invited Fluff's mother to tea and made fast friends with her. Fluff and I began to share my perambulator, and she's been my shadow ever since."

"A malevolent shadow, if I might say. She's obviously jealous of you."

Lazuli shrugged. "If I gave up on her, she'd have no one."

"That explains a lot. I appreciate you even more, Laz." He drew close and tentatively touched her cheek. "I've missed you."

"It's only been two days since you last saw me." Lazuli gently removed his hand and leaned demurely back.

"An eternity, you mean."

"Yes. An eternity." They gazed at one another for a long moment. Oak was having a hard time breathing and he didn't think it was the dust.

"Lazuli, I love — " Oak's throat closed off.

"Yes?"

"You – your dress."

Lazuli raised a manicured eyebrow. "You were going to say something else, Oak."

"Wh-what makes you think that?"

"Oak, what if I told you I love you, too. Would that scare you?"

Scare me? He pulled on his collar. "It would petrify me, but I'd feel worse if it weren't true." Oak felt a sudden rush of emotion and before he could stop himself, he'd crushed Lazuli to his chest. "As a matter of fact, Lazuli, I would simply perish if it weren't true!"

"Oak," Lazuli gasped, "could you let go? I can't breathe. Ooh, thank you." She took a deep breath.

"I'm sorry."

She sandwiched Oak's face between her hands and studied his eyes. "I do love you, Oak. With all my heart." She lightly kissed his lips.

Ah, such exquisite sweetness. "Then I love you, too," said Oak, with enthusiasm.

"*And* my dress?" Lazuli grinned.

"Your dress, too. All of you." His face felt hot. "So, my, er, dear. Where do we go from here?"

Lazuli thought a moment. "Our parents won't let us get married this young, you know."

"And I still need to become a reporter and you still need to become a veterinarian."

"I'm beginning to rethink that, Oak. How would you like a botanist for a wife?"

"Whatever toots your horn, dear."

"Four years then. That should give me plenty of time to plan the most spectacular wedding New York has ever seen!" She gazed at Oak intently.

"Uh, Laz, that reminds me. I have a confession to make. I hope it doesn't change your mind about me . . . us."

Lazuli paused. "I think I'm past the place where anything you say would affect my love for you — unless you're about to tell me there's another girl hidden away somewhere."

Oak chuckled. "Lazuli Waters, there has never been anyone but you in my heart, nor will there ever be anyone but you."

"Well, then, I'm ready to listen."

The time had come for him to share his news, the decision he'd been thinking about for weeks, trying to find the choice that he would never regret, that would guide the direction of not only his life, but also Lazuli's. "I want to be a reporter, but I don't want to go to New York. I want to come back to Grand Junction and make a difference here. I-I hope you aren't disappointed."

Lazuli's mouth formed a satisfied smile. "Why should I be? I've known for a while. Oak, are you always going to be this slow with decisions? Because if you are, we need to talk. Of course, my family will be pleased, especially Grandmama. They all want to be a part of our children's lives. I hope we have a girl first . . . "

"Yowzah! I just thought of something."

"What is it?"

"This means I'm going to be related to Fluff!"

Chapter Twelve

"Run, Grace, like the wind!" Robert and Eulila cheered their daughter on as she hop-skipped with her pig-tailed friend. "Come on, Catherine, you can do it!"

When Oak and Lazuli finally returned to the crowd, their virtue still intact, the three-legged races were going. They watched the race for a short time, but Oak was voraciously hungry and dropped by the Miller blanket to see if any food was left. His family had thoughtfully saved a little of everything. Oak offered a meatloaf sandwich to Lazuli, but she turned it down.

"I'm on a diet."

Oak looked at her like she was crazy. "But — " Lazuli's expression squelched any further comment.

"There are two theories to arguing with a woman, Oak. Neither work."

"Dalton!" Oak clapped his friend on his shoulder. "I thought this party was only for Fair employees and their families. What are you doing here?"

"We're friends of the Gesbergs."

He pointed to his family as they set out their picnic. Orus and Maud were laughing at something together.

"The Gesbergs asked us to come, but I can leave if you don't want me here." He started to turn away, clearly expecting to be stopped.

"Stay and celebrate. There's so much to celebrate." He winked at Lazuli.

"Am I ever going to be introduced to this beautiful lady?" Dalton took Lazuli's hand and kissed it.

"I'm still teaching him manners," she said. "Lazuli Waters."

"Charmed."

"I'm sure."

Dalton toggled his eyebrows at Oak. "Does she have a sister? Sylvia gave my pin back."

Oak started to say something, but Lazuli interrupted. She took Dalton's arm and said, "Why, yes, I do. A lovely girl. Would you like to meet her?"

Dalton patted his heart as Lazuli led him away. Oak shook his head and chuckled; Dalton was going to make a great roommate.

When it got dark John Gesberg called everyone to the fire, crackling pleasantly. People cheerfully gathered around and sat on the logs that outlined the perimeter.

Oak walked over to the fire with Lazuli, Dalton, and the ever-present Fluff. Dalton seemed to be enjoying Fluff's company immensely. She hadn't stopped talking since they'd been introduced, and he seemed to listen with great interest. Oak took him aside before they sat down and asked why the attention.

"Fascinating woman. She's going in a future book, if I have anything to say about it. Got to get back to work." Dalton hopped over the log and sat next to Fluff. Amazed, Oak and Lazuli joined them.

"Close your mouth, dear," Eulila said as she and his father appeared next to Oak. They greeted Lazuli.

"Mother, I haven't seen you two all evening."

"Your father and I took a long walk. Did you know there are cliffs just over there?" She pointed vaguely past the farmhouse. "And caves? We found one, and, um, watched the sunset. Didn't we, dear?"

Her husband's face reddened in the firelight. "Yes. An amazing sunset!"

Oak reached over and straightened the collar on his mother's dress. "Some sunsets are unforgettable." He turned his gaze to the crackling fire and smiled.

The sing-along started with "For Me And My Gal," followed by "Bill Bailey." Everyone rocked side to side in unison. When the next song "You're the Cream in My Coffee" started, Eulila asked, "Where's Grace?"

> *You're the cream in my coffee*
> *You're the salt in my stew . . .*

"Last I saw, she was winning the three-legged race." Standing up, Oak stretched to see as many faces as he could. "There she is, Mother, way over there, by Lillian Gesberg."

"I better go get her. The fireworks will be starting soon."

> *You will always be*
> *My 'necessity'*
> *I'd be lost without you . . .*

"We can get her. You just enjoy the fire. Laz?" On the way there, Lazuli stumbled over a rock in the dark and Oak caught her.

"Will you always be my hero?"

"It's my destiny." Oak grabbed Lazuli and danced with her. Along with the crowd he sang:

> *You're the starch in my collar*
> *You're the lace in my shoe*
> *You will always be*
> *My 'necessity'*
> *I'd be lost without you.*

"You don't say?" She stopped and pulled him to her with force. She kissed him so passionately it left Oak with goose bumps. "That had better hold you for four years!"

"I believe if any kiss could, it would be that one." He wiped the sweat from his top lip. "Hello, Grace. Did Lillian fall asleep?"

Grace jumped up, her round eyes brimming over with tears. "I think something's wrong with her. We were talking about the baby and she was so happy. Then she grabbed her tummy and groaned. Then she just — fell over. Did I do something to hurt her?"

Lazuli was at Lillian's side in a second. She kneeled down and gently moved her so she could see Lillian's face. Her eyes were closed, eyelashes brushing her damp cheeks. Lazuli listened to her breathing. "She's alive. When did this happen, Grace?"

"Just a minute ago. Is she going to be all right?" Lazuli gave Oak a look.

"Sure, sis, she'll be fine. Let's go find Mother and see if she can't dry your eyes, okey-dokey?" Oak mouthed over Grace's head, "I'll get Art."

The sing-along was still going, the night air filled with reedy, sonorous, raspy, childlike, happy voices. It made an unusual musical score for the drama going on fifty feet away in the semi-dark.

Oak dropped Grace off with their parents, then found Art. Soon there was a small core of people bending over Lillian, mostly family. The brothers Art, Carl, Leslie, and Harold helped John carry Lillian into the farmhouse. Ana, Harold's wife, held her daughter's hand, while Lazuli comforted Agnes, who covered her mouth with her hand. William Moyer's diminutive figure flickered in the shadows as the distant fire danced across his back.

The last song, "Secondhand Rose," ended and everyone's attention turned to the fireworks. Laughter punctuated the festive mood. Leonard Anderegg, with Wilma and little Betty by his side, set off the first rocket. It cracked loudly and then exploded over-head. Everyone cried out in delight.

Oak and Lazuli gravitated to each other and embraced. "She said, 'My baby.' Oh, Oak," Lazuli buried her face in his shoulder. "It's too sad!"

Holding her close, he looked at the scene around him. Sitting close together on a log, Evan settled a blanket around Margaret's shoulders. In spite of their recent loss, they looked peaceful. Oak's parents weren't even watching the fireworks; they only had eyes for each other. Grace's new friend, Catherine, sat next to her listening intently and patting her shoulder. Fluff had Dalton's complete attention and both seemed to be enjoying their conversation. And in the nearby house a story still unfolding, its end not yet written . . .

Tragedy and revelation, compassion and restoration, and sorrow overcome and transformed — just some of the precious threads woven into this small pioneer town on the edge of the high desert.

How Oak loved Grand Junction.

"Last Sunday, Pastor Jim told our congregation that life is like a tapestry." Lazuli raised her face to Oak, her eyes searching for comfort. He tenderly brushed a tear away with his thumb. "From underneath, he said, the world can seem jumbled and non-sensical; but from heaven, the Weaver sees His woven story in all its glorious patterns and colors." Oak looked at the farmhouse. "He said when nothing makes sense, trust that it makes sense to God, and it'll be okay."

Lazuli sniffed. "In spite of the craziness, life *is* worth liv-ing, isn't it?"

Oak gathered her into his arms. "Yes, my love. We must always believe it is."

Giml
By Peggy Godfrey

This aching in my chest
These tears, this confusion
And you know how poets are!!
They want a name for everything.
It's been chaos in my head and heart
A struggle to push beyond the tears
And it came to me this morning.
Weaning! That's what it is
The goal of that intimate nurture
Of a loved one
The moving beyond
That life-giving expression of love
To another fullness of love
One where a spirit of adventure
Is free to set the pace
Where wings spread to fly
High and far away
Songs are cast upon the winds
And love returns to love by choice.

Ah, the sweetness of seeing the hope unfold
And the pain of heavy breasts
Waiting for the milk to dry up.

The Hebrew letter Giml means nurturing not for
dependence,but for the sake of weaning.
Peggy Godfrey gave birth to a stillborn baby girl in 1974.

The Real Story

Newborn Baby's Mummified Body
Found By Three Exploring Boys
The Daily Sentinel article

Dec. 31 The casket and mummified body of a
newborn infant believed to have been buried 25 to 50
years ago was found by three exploring youths
Thursday about 4p.m. in a cave about two miles south
of the Whitewater dump . . .

December 30, 1971, the three Grandbouche boys, Jay (age 13), Scott (age 9), and Todd (age 6), were getting under their mother, Barbara's, feet. Near the end of school's winter break, everyone was suffering from cabin fever. Barbara strongly suggested the boys do something outside since it was sunny and her sanity was waning.

So after stocking up on food, coats, and hopes of finding Indian artifacts or other treasure, the three brothers set off across Highway 50. They jumped over the dry canal and hiked across the loamy earth to the bluffs overlooking the Gunnison River.

It would be a day they'd never forget.

Dusk was etching its way across the sky when Barbara started looking for the boys' return. It got darker and she kept checking the kitchen window for any sign of them. Nothing. Just when she was beginning to worry, three very excited boys came running up the driveway.

Their words tumbled out in a jumble. At first Barbara couldn't believe their story. A casket with a baby found in a cave? Surely they were mistaken! At the boys' insistence their father, George, called the sheriff's office with the news. The time was 5:43 p.m.

A caravan of sheriff's deputies, both on and off duty, and the coroner followed George Grandbouche and his family as they drove to the cave. Seeing all the colored lights flashing brightly in his rearview mirror George said, "Boy, you guys had better be telling the truth or you're in really big trouble!"

Enthusiastically his sons reassured him.

When the cars pulled in front of the rock outcropping where the cave was they all got out. Deputies Ben Martinez and Earl Sawyer and the Mesa County coroner, William Doell, were the investigators.

They assessed the situation and decided to send the boys up to the cave to retrieve the casket. Barbara went with them, carrying a camera. Before the boys brought the casket down she'd taken several photos to memorialize the moment.

Jay and his brothers carefully trekked the tiny casket over the boulders until they laid it at the feet of the deputies. Everyone gathered around as the lid was removed.

There, nestled on creamy folds of aged muslin, lay the mummified remains of a little girl. Her head, dark hair feathered across her scalp, was close to the right end of the casket. She lay on her left side as if sleeping, wrapped in thin cotton batting. The length of her body was about twelve inches.

The boys were asked to tell their story.

They shared how they'd been looking for Indian artifacts all day. Around four p.m. they were cold and hungry so they climbed to a cave they were familiar with to eat and get warm. In the middle of the cave was a rectangular rock about two feet tall. The boys had always used it as a table.

While eating, Jay tossed a stone at their "table." The action produced a hollow sound and the brothers realized something was there. This ignited their hopes of buried treasure as they'd heard outlaws might have hidden in the area long ago. Chipping away at the rock they realized it wasn't a rock at all, but a large object covered in a thick crust of adobe-mud made from rocks and dirt that had dried. They weren't making very good progress despite their labor so Jay and Scott went down to the railroad tracks to find a couple of spikes. As they went down, Todd hollered that he'd managed to break off a sizeable chunk and had unearthed wood.

The older boys returned quickly with spikes and they chipped away in earnest. Their efforts were rewarded when a wooden box was revealed underneath the broken adobe.

The box had a slatted lid nailed on and between the slats a chest could be seen. Jay quickly pulled on the slats until they splintered. The brothers savored the moment before Jay reached in and removed the chest. A well built octagonal, its dimensions were about two feet long and a foot-and-a-half tall. It had a four-tiered lid and the outside was covered in yellowed cloth. Not your usual outlaw treasure chest but who were they to argue? Visions of golden coins and glittering jewelry danced before their eyes.

Jay directed Todd to open the chest and, with trembling hands, he did. His nose was near the edge of the lid, and when it came off he complained, "Ew, that smells bad!"

The boys didn't know what exactly they'd found when the lid was off. But it wasn't outlaw treasure. It looked more like — a tiny body.

Jay picked up the lid again. Earlier he'd noticed a metal plate attached to it. Perhaps it could explain the chest's unusual contents. A dark gray patina covered the fancy calligraphy. It said, *Our Darling*.

Their eyes widened as they realized what they'd unearthed. They had to tell someone!

According to *The Daily Sentinel* article written the day after the discovery, the casket was taken to morticians to determine how old the casket was. It was manufactured, the mortuary reported to Dr. Doell, and was probably buried between twenty-five and fifty years ago. Cast-iron handles on the sides helped determine the age as well as the round nails used to join the box.

Dr. Doell weighed the baby at about five pounds and guessed she had died at birth. He told the *Sentinel* that authorities had done about as much as they could to determine the age of baby and casket.

Five months passed as the police, sheriff's office, coroner's office and the Grandbouche family tried to learn the baby's identity. The story went out on the Associated Press wire, making the news in Denver and most likely on a national level.

No one came forward to claim Our Darling.

Martin's Mortuary kept the baby until May 1972, when the Grandbouche family and other interested parties decided the little girl needed to be reburied. A collection was taken up by employees at the Atomic Energy Commission compound where George Grandbouche worked. The city of Grand Junction agreed to open a grave in the Orchard Mesa Cemetery and provide perpetual care for $70. With AEC donations and money raised by Jay, Scott, and Todd, the fees were taken care of. Even the coroner, William Doell, contributed to the fund.

Our Darling was reburied May 11, 1972.

Snyder Memorials provided the headstone. It said:

OUR DARLING
FOUND IN A CAVE
S.W. OF WHITEWATER
DEC. 1971
INFANT UNKNOWN
BURIAL APPX. 1900-1920

Orchard Mesa Cemetery is where I was first introduced to Our Darling, while on a Dave Fishell tour one summer day in 1999.

After learning the Grandbouches lived nearby, I got home from the cemetery and looked up their phone number. Barbara agreed to let me interview her and Jay, who was living with her, the next day. When I got there I was extremely pleased that Barbara had many pictures of the cave, the boys in the cave, the casket, the baby, the funeral, and articles about Our Darling and her discovery.

Mother and son related to me and my tape recorder what had happened that day. I found out that several details hadn't made the news articles or Fishell's cemetery tour. Avidly I listened to their story, taking notes and recording.

Some of the details I didn't know included the fact that Dr. Doell had only done a cursory examination of the body. He'd determined she had not died under suspicious circumstances as there was nothing to indicate broken bones or trauma. And by sight alone, he had determined the baby was Caucasian.

Barbara recounted a few details about the casket. Its lining was made of satin that was worn and yellowed, and its outside was covered in a textured fabric.

I asked her about the discrepancy of the date on the tombstone. It was not the original estimation of Our Darling's death and burial. The *Sentinel* had reported the mortuary and coroner had set her death between twenty-five and fifty years ago — that was between 1922 and 1947 — so perhaps in the five-month interim something had changed. Barbara only remembered that the 1900 to 1920 time frame was the final conclusion by the mortuary.

Jay filled me in on his experiences as one of the discoverers. His story was typical of brothers on an adventure and their excitement at discovering something so unusual. He described the area, mentioning a coal mine that could be seen across from the cave. There were rock foundations at the base of the outcropping that held the cave, with more foundations some distance away.

I made a note to myself to check these out.

Jay offered to lead me to the cave sometime, saying it would take several hours to hike there. When Our Darling was first discovered, he explained, one could drive to that area by going through the dump, but that route was closed off now. I readily agreed to the hike and asked if Dave Fishell, who was very interested, could come along. No problem.

Unfortunately when I got home from my interview with Jay and Barbara, I found my little recorder hadn't worked properly and I had to recount their stories from memory onto the blank tape. This would later be a deep disappointment to the Grandbouche family and me.

Although I was working on my first book, *Stained Glass Rose*, I wanted Our Darling's story to be next. I began a file at home with copies of the pictures, articles, and the recordings. I made a list of things to do, including checking out the coal mine and rock foundations. Either one could prove important in discovering Our Darling's identity.

After *Stained Glass Rose* was published two-and-a-half years later, I began in earnest to research Our Darling's story. I had my work cut out for me.

Jay Grandbouche had told me that sometime after the discovery, someone thought those rock foundations could be a place called "Nigger Flats," a poor community of blacks that lived outside the city limits during the first part of the century. With the location of the grave, the proximity of Nigger Flats, the lack of name, and no one coming forward to claim Our Darling, it occurred to me this baby might have been illegitimate.

Perhaps she was the product of an illicit relationship between a handsome, wealthy, but misunderstood married man and a compassionate, poor, but beautiful maid. Maybe there was a dedicated black nanny or cook involved that arranged to have the baby, who died tragically, buried above Nigger Flats, the closed-to-everyone-but-would-make-an-exception-in-Our-Darling's-case community. My writer's mentality came up with all sorts of soap opera scenarios, but before my imagination started throwing in heaving breasts and throbbing, er, hearts, I decided to start with the facts.

The first thing I did was contact longtime Whitewater resident Bud Bradbury, who drew me a map of where Nigger Flats had been. After driving to that location, I could see it wasn't anywhere near the cave. So much for melodrama . . .

Then I called Jay Grandbouche to see if we could hike to the cave soon. If I saw the surroundings, maybe I could add some dimension to his memories. Our schedules conflicted, but we decided to go after hunting season was over, sometime late fall 2002 or early spring 2003.

Next, I started with the pictures of Our Darling. I figured if I could date the casket more accurately, I could pinpoint the time of her death. With even a decade to go by, I could scour the newspapers, albeit tedious work, for the untimely death of a little girl.

I blew up color copies of the casket, both closed and with the lid open and the baby visible. I put together a synopsis of what I knew so far and then called Mike Blackburn of Callahan-

Edfast Mortuary. I also called the now-named Martin Mortuary and Crematory to see if they could find Our Darling's records since they had originally determined the casket's age.

Mike Blackburn, who has a great sense of humor, met with me and took a look at the pictures. He couldn't specifically date the casket, but he said it probably was produced around the late 1910s, possibly to accommodate the infant deaths during the flu epidemic of 1918. He said many mortuaries back then tended to buy up warehouses full of caskets, especially if they were on sale. It might take several decades to use them all, but they would never go to waste. There would always be the dead to use them.

To the question of whether one could bury a body anywhere, Mike said that today you need a permit to bury someone in a certain place, but back then there had been no such policies in place. Therefore if a baby died it wouldn't have to be buried in a cemetery. It could be buried next to one's garden or, yes, in a cave. More common for the time, many infants didn't even get a funeral.

I asked about a death certificate, and Mike told me that if an infant died at home, without a doctor attending, there would be no certificate. And many died at home, especially in outlying areas. The length of time it would take for a doctor to make an emergency house call or a sick person to get to a hospital contributed to a high infant mortality rate.

One more thing Mike told me was Our Darling's casket was a costly one, based on the tiers of the lid. The more tiers, the more expensive.

Mike's information was helpful, but it was imperative the casket be dated as precisely as possible if I was going to find Our Darling's identity. Mike suggested I go online and visit a funeral museum. A funeral museum? I'd never heard of such a thing.

Sure enough, I found the Museum of Funeral Customs in Springfield, Illinois. Its director is Jon Austin. To my inquiry, he requested I fax pictures, articles, and synopsis of Our Darling's story to him. The faxed pictures were fuzzy, and Jon asked if I could send the color pictures by mail and he'd look at them.

The faxed articles were readable, fortunately. After a quick perusal, Jon emailed that the cast-iron handles mentioned didn't make sense to him. His museum had collected many handles of 19th and 20th century origin, and he'd seen almost none that were cast-iron. He wrote:

> *"By the later 19th century, most handles were being made of zinc or white metal as were the name plates and other fittings."*

I sent the pictures by overnight delivery along with other information Jon had requested, such as what the lining fabric and exterior casket cloth looked like. I emphasized my desire to date the casket.

After Jon received the color pictures, he emailed back. Based on his experiences with different burials, it was his opinion Our Darling had not been a random burial, but she had been loved deeply and the cave location had been chosen carefully.

He offered some insight into the casket, too.

> *"My thought is that the plank box that you described was probably the shipping crate that had carried the casket from the manufacturers to the under-taker, who prepared the remains."*

Jon continued his research and less than a week later, he wrote:

"I've not found identical matches among our collections of casket handles and name plates. I have found a nearly identical photo in a casket catalog even down to the fabric covering. The problem is that our catalog is undated . . . "

And two weeks and more research later:

"Because of the shape, the container is properly called a 'casket' and not a 'coffin.' It appears to be a 'cloth-covered octagon' made of wood that was produced in a factory. The interior may also be a factory production or it could have been upholstered by the funeral director.

The handles are probably zinc or white metal, or they may have been painted or silver-plated. The design motif is likely to be a crouching lamb above a bale. Above the lamb, it appears that there are clouds or solar rays. Similar handles in the collection have either a cast bale or a functioning bale that would swivel. The handles may not have been functional.

This casket would have been small enough (and lightweight) that one person could have carried it.

The red dots on the handles were probably the nails used to mount them on the box. The metal plate appears to be a stock item, the "Our Darling" motto standard. It is most likely that the motto would have run on a single line.

The fabric casket covering doesn't appear to have a pile (like plush or velvet) but instead had a woven texture in a diamond pattern. The stripe up the end is a piece of braid used to hide the butted edges of the

*fabric . . . They call the fabric, 'P.K.,' which I believe is
a corruption of the word, 'pique,' and that matches what
I see in your photos."*

The catalog Jon drew this information from was undated
but looked to him like it circulated around the 1910s.

Jon also suggested I check property records to see who
owned the land where the cave sits. He was not able to find any
more information to help me, but I felt I had an exciting start,
even though his information generated more questions.

Another funeral museum, in Houston, said they had a
similar casket in a 1933 catalog, but my request for a picture
was not answered.

I did some research on nails, thinking I could refine the dating of the casket by the "round nails" reported in the *Sentinel* article, and what I assumed Jon's "red dots on the handles" were. I
learned that round nails had been introduced, depending on the
website you visited, between 1890 and 1910.

I also found a site online about Charles A. Rickett, founder
of Maplewood Cemetery in Brownington, Osage Township,
Henry County, Missouri. He was undertaker there from 1904 to
1946, and sold Our Darling's type of casket. His sales ledger for
those years was listed and as early as 1904, an adult-sized white
"PK" casket had been sold. On January 26, 1906, one white PK
casket, size 3'0", had been sold for $14. This was a child's casket.
Over the next twenty-five years various children's white PK caskets, ranging in sizes from 2'0" to 4'0", were sold. The prices for
size 2'0" (the size of Our Darling's) ranged from $8 to $16. Not
all were covered in PK. Some were covered in "lambskin," others
in "plush," and at least one in something defined as "H." I
stopped at 1931, where in January, one 2'0" white PK casket was
sold to Steve Stevens for $11.

I wondered how Martin's Mortuary came up with their calculations only one day after the discovery when the funeral museum, with a plethora of information at their fingertips, had a hard time dating the casket. Maybe Martin's had been familiar with that type of casket.

Time to ask. I faxed LaNora Trujillo at Martin Mortuary with pictures, etc., and asked if they could find Our Darling's records.

In the meantime, I attended a Seventh Street Home Tour and met Marilyn Olson, granddaughter of Clyde Martin, founder of Martin's Mortuary. After telling her I was a writer of Grand Junction histories and mysteries, I explained what my next book was about. I asked if her grandfather would have upholstered a casket's interior, which Jon Austin had suggested was a possibility. Marilyn was pretty sure he did not. I asked if she knew whom the mortuary had bought their caskets from in the 1920s. She said, while her family owned the mortuary, all their caskets and coffins had been bought from one company, Law and Sons, out of Denver.

Aha! Maybe they had some old catalogs! Sigh . . . they were out of business.

After a few days, Paula Maley, at Martin Mortuary, called me. They couldn't find any record of the baby having been there. She suggested Dr. Doell, the coroner, might have taken the file with him after the baby was buried.

Research on Dr. William Doell told me he had moved to Denver decades ago. A check with AOL's white pages and the Social Security Death Index produced no William Doell. Given his probable age, he was likely in a rest home or living with relatives — and difficult to trace.

When I tried to find Ben Martinez and Earl Sawyer, the sheriff's deputies who investigated the case, I discovered they had both passed away.

I was discouraged. Too many dead ends (no pun intended). Several events occurred the winter of 2003.

On January 19, Jay Grandbouche, aged 44, tragically died of a heart attack. He left behind four sons, his mother and two brothers. I remembered I had recorded Jay and I thought I could make a CD with his words on it and give it to his family as a memento. When I checked the interview tape, my own voice reminded me that it had not worked. What a time for technology to fail.

Jay's untimely death seemed a poignant reminder that time stands still for no man. I'd put it off long enough. After a decent interval I contacted Jay's youngest brother, Todd, and asked him to help me find Our Darling's cave. He was unable to guide me that weekend, but drew a map of its location. As the crow flies on 29 1/2 Road to the Gunnison River, it was not that far. Unfortunately one can't get there as the crow flies, so I was lucky to find a man, Clint Dawson, who was familiar with the area. On a spring Saturday, Clint guided my husband, Ben, and me over the bluffs to the cave.

It was a very touching moment for me when I sat down at its entrance. I imagined the small group of mourners carrying the crate with its casket over the boulders, and clearing the dirt away from the cave's floor before setting their precious cargo down. I imagined one of the mourners bringing up bucketfuls of river water to make the adobe to entomb the crate. I almost heard the weeping and the solemn, loving words dedicating Our Darling's soul into her Maker's arms.

It took over two hours to hike there and forty-five minutes to meet Clint's wife, Janell, at the dump for the ride home. We all were tired, but I was excited.

Monday morning I was on the phone to Dale Williams at Abstract & Title Company. After hearing my reasons for requesting a title search, he agreed to help, gratis. Bless his heart. A couple of weeks later he called.

Two men had patented that area, Lots 4-7, Section 8. Lots 5-7 were patented by Harris M. Kissell in September 1912, and Lot 4 was patented by James U. Harris in December 1912. Both men lived in Grand Junction, though James Harris was a rancher. Kissell was a "groundsman" for the telephone and telegraph company, according to the 1912 city directory. There was no indication either ever lived by the cave or worked that coal mine.

Checking their family's obituaries, one had lost a three-month old daughter, but she'd been buried in the Palisade cemetery. I still didn't rule out the possibility that a baby might have died at home and been buried at the cave, even though not reported in the obituaries.

I'd also discovered there was no official birth or death pages in the early newspapers. Notices were placed where there was room and that could be anywhere. Since some of the microfiche had smudged pages, I could have easily missed a baby's death notice on my search through the newspapers.

Searching property records at the clerk and recorder's office, it was apparent none of the property owners, before it was sold to Mesa County in the 1970s, acknowledged the foundations at the foot of the rock outcropping near the cave. Additionally, a search through a list of coal mines in our county made no mention of a mine across from the cave, even though one had existed.

There was the possibility of pre-1912 squatters working the mine, but there were no records to back that theory up. I decided to dismiss the idea of squatters. The foundations were simply stones laid on top of each other, about a foot or two high, and no other "housing" materials littered the area. The Grandbouche boys had many contemporaries who had explored that area, and the foundations could have simply been from play.

When I was growing up, my sister and I had done something similar with smaller rocks in a field next to us. We arranged the stones into "rooms" and then played "house."

So what I could surmise at this point in time was that the casket was probably made between 1906 and 1933, that it was one of the more expensive (by 1920s terms) caskets, and that Our Darling's burial in a cave had been an act of love, not shame. I also believed she was the child of someone who was very familiar with the area and that the cave had special meaning.

I decided it was time to start collecting information on Grand Junction and Orchard Mesa. I knew many hours of reading lay ahead and I wanted to get started: I just needed a year to begin!

Don't laugh, but I prayed about it. I figured man may not know a thing about Our Darling, but God surely knew it all. After praying, I strongly felt I should start looking in the 1920s.

I'd always dreamed of honoring, through my writing, William Moyer, our most progressive leader of early Grand Junction. I'd also wanted to learn more about Dalton Trumbo, our most famous, or infamous, citizen. A third interest was the builder of the concrete block house on Orchard Mesa, mainly because it looked old and was located somewhat near the Gunnison River and Our Darling's burial cave.

Through research, I found Dalton Trumbo had left Grand Junction in 1924, Moyer's Fair Store was booming at that time, and a man named J.B. Gesberg had built the concrete block house on Orchard Mesa — and was also a longtime manager at the Fair Store. 1924 it was.

I started with J.B. Gesberg. Through research I learned he had lived in three homes on Orchard Mesa before he died in 1933. Before 1908, when the beautiful ten-room concrete home had been built, he and his wife, Agnes, lived across from Lincoln

School, close to Four Corners. J.B. worked at the Fair Store and Agnes took in boarders until the family moved to their new home at present-day 27 and B 1/2 Roads.

At the library I found an oral history interview taken with Carl Gesberg, the second youngest son. It filled in some blanks. Carl remembered that when the concrete block house was built, it was the only Orchard Mesa home with running water. In their attic was a tank that J.B. filled with artesian water from the well at the cemetery, and gravity would distribute it throughout the house. It was also the house with the dreaded enema machine his father had invented, which I mention in the story.

Carl said his brothers liked the two-story farmhouse they moved into next the best. In the early 1910s, J.B. built a farmhouse overlooking the Gunnison River. Carl recounted in his oral history that he and his brothers had often explored the river and the bluffs overlooking it.

Now I was getting somewhere. I had a family that lived close to Our Darling's cave and like the Grandbouche boys, the Gesberg brothers had explored the Gunnison River bluffs regularly. They could have found and took shelter in Our Darling's cave on numerous occasions. And it could have had great meaning to one of those brothers.

My next question was, did any of those boys grow up, marry, and live on Orchard Mesa? Did any lose a child?

At the Mesa County Public Library, I found the obituaries of all four sons as well as their parents. The whole family had lived, married, and been buried in Grand Junction, and every one of them had lived on Orchard Mesa for some, if not most, of their adult life.

By now, the characters for the fictional story of *Our Darling* began developing themselves. I find my characters start taking on a life of their own after I build their sketches. Oak

Miller crafted himself into a recent graduate of Grand Junction High School who wanted to make a difference in the world and he had chosen the profession of a reporter to accomplish that. That was the same profession Dalton Trumbo had been in throughout high school.

Trumbo had been a successful reporter for *The Daily Sentinel* and a correspondent for the Denver papers. With both Oak and Dalton as reporters, I needed to get into their minds if I was going to write from their perspectives.

A phone call to Gary Harmon, a news reporter at *The Daily Sentinel,* got me an appointment to spend part of a Friday with him. Gary is a no-nonsense kind of man, but he has a melliflu-ous vocabulary. I caught the tail end of his midmorning whirl-wind and bounced along to the courthouse, where we sat in on a murder trial; then to a working lunch; then to a reception at the dinosaur museum in Fruita. Close to four p.m., I followed Gary back to the *Sentinel* for a quick introduction to the various depart-ment heads and then I watched him put together several articles under a five p.m. deadline.

My favorite part of the day was eating lunch at City Market, where the local legal scuttlebutt was passed around like salt and pepper.

There I met Bob Thorpe who, along with his wife, is a bail bondsmen. When Bob found out I was writing about Our Darling, he said he'd heard Bob Silva talk about being part of an investigation involving a baby in a casket. That evening, he had Bob call me.

Bob Silva, an ex-sheriff's deputy, and I met over coffee at Barnes and Noble. He'd investigated a baby that had been found in a casket some decades back. He described what she'd looked like, what she was wearing, and the note (!) that was found in the casket. Bob even remembered what the note said: something like,

"I am so sorry I won't get to see you grow up." He also remembered that Mesa County Coroner Alex Thompson had been especially tender with the case. I remarked that I hadn't known another coroner, other than Doell, had been involved.

Bob Silva's news was exciting to me, especially the note. None of this was mentioned when I'd spoken to the Grandbouches. The authorities must have been privy to unreleased details.

The next day, I called the Mesa County Sheriff's Office and talked to their spokesperson, Janet Prell, who requested an archives search for the incident report of Our Darling. Later, I got a call from Janet who had the report on her desk and would make a copy for me. I was down there in a few minutes.

It was a "skeleton" report, basically stating that two miles southwest of the Whitewater Dump, George Grandbouche reported his three sons had found a casket buried in a cave. The casket was a wooden box, buried with mortar (the adobe tomb) sealing it and contained the mummified remains of an infant. The only officers listed were Earl Sawyer and Ben Martinez. No Bob Silva. No Alex Thompson.

I checked out Thompson's stint as coroner and he didn't start until after 1972. Obviously, the dead baby that Bob Silva had investigated was another, similar case, but not Our Darling's. Rats!

My research was riddled with dead ends, red herrings, unknowns, and tantalizing leads, but I was determined, more than ever, to find Our Darling's identity. By now she was like family.

At this time I was juggling several projects. I was developing my characters and laying out plot lines. I was collecting information about Grand Junction's buildings and people in the 1920s.

Judy Prosser-Armstrong, Sissy Williams, Dave Fishell, and Dave Sundal at the Museum of Western Colorado were very helpful in my endeavors to recreate the Roaring Twenties. Dave Sundal had actually visited the elder Dalton Trumbo in California, shortly before he died.

Carol Newton, landlady of the Fair building, let me and Chris Brown, of Brown's Cycles, explore its abandoned second floor and basement. The firm, A.G. Edwards and Sons, uses the first floor now and guards the access to the second floor, elevator room, and roof. Carol gave us permission to go upstairs.

Somewhere I'd heard the Fair elevator was supposed to have been the first in town. I'd heard the elevator at St. Mary's on Colorado Avenue had also been the first. When Chris and I climbed the (very) steep stairs to the elevator room, there was a 1922 "Olof Reverse Phase Relay" (I'm assuming a type of elevator motor) made by the Otis Elevator Company of New York. Someday I'll have to figure out if this was the first in town.

To get to the basement, we had to take our shoes off and go through the Academy of Yoga on 5th Street and walk down the stairs. The basement was especially exciting.

I knew the basement had first been used by the Fair Store, and later by Montgomery Ward's. Near the Main Street-side wall, a beautiful wooden staircase descended elegantly from the ceiling, where the entrance had been blocked off. Chris Brown said he felt like we'd discovered the sunken *Titanic*. He's so funny.

Kathy Jordan, of *The Daily Sentinel*, helped me understand 1920s Grand Junction. She invited me to sit a spell on her Victorian porch in the tony historical district and get the feel of a "small town on a Sunday afternoon." She helped me "see" Walter Walker, the publisher of *The Daily Sentinel*, and how the newspaper had been run. She also knew a lot about Dalton Trumbo.

I was fortunate enough to read a copy of Dalton Trumbo's book, *Eclipse*. Of course, me being desensitized by today's standard of bad-mouthing, *Eclipse* could be a Disney script for all its punch.

It was written in the early 1930s, published in 1935 by a London house, and derided by most of Grand Junction's citizens for decades. Many felt the book insulted the townspeople; they felt Trumbo had written his book because of sour grapes over his father being fired by Bert Benge, the Shoe Man, in November 1924.

Orus Trumbo could be very curt and he probably was not the best of salesmen. After his dismissal, he was not able to find work, so in the spring of 1925, he and his family moved to California in hopes of finding a job. Dalton quit college and followed them that summer. He came through Grand Junction to pick up belongings left behind and then headed west. He didn't go back to college for nearly ten years. His biography, *Trumbo*, by Bruce Cook, said he never returned to Grand Junction.

Regarding "sour grapes," after reading *Trumbo*, I think he may indeed have been trying to slay some childhood dragons through his writing. I also think he realized his father had his strong and weak points.

I found *Eclipse* an interesting read. Knowing that Trumbo had left Grand Junction in 1924, many of his memories of this town, written in great detail in *Eclipse*, were probably the clearest picture of what it actually looked like. After all, he'd been trained as a reporter. He'd fictionalized and renamed the townspeople, the town's name, and its businesses, and created some situations and descriptions that were entirely fictional, but Grand Junction was still highly recognizable.

The character of John Abbott, really William Moyer some say, only solidified my idea that Moyer was a top-notch man. There were many mentions of "Abbott's" benevolence to his town, including helping a girl who'd gotten herself pregnant by paying for her expenses, and acting as financial advisor for a local madam.

On top of immersing myself in 1924 Grand Junction via the *Sentinel* newspapers, *Eclipse*, and personal interviews, I continued to learn more about the Gesbergs. Little tidbits, such as parties attended or thrown, illnesses suffered, and other news would appear in the Orchard Mesa correspondent column. When I looked in the phone book to see if any relatives still lived in Grand Junction, there was only one Gesberg listed.

Wallace "Bud" Gesberg lived two blocks away from me. After trying to contact him unsuccessfully by phone for a couple of days, I dropped a note by, asking him to call.

As it turned out, I'd left the note on the wrong door, but that wound up being good. The Gesbergs had been out of town and if I'd put the note on the correct door, it probably would have blown away. The good neighbors made sure Bud got my note when he and his wife returned home. He called me, and though I was still in curlers and face cream, you never saw anyone move so fast! Several minutes later, I was knocking on their door.

Here I had a real breakthrough. Bud had some old pictures he'd planned on giving to the trash collectors the next day. Talk about timing!

Because of my research, I recognized a lot of the people in the pictures and was especially pleased to see a few of Art Gesberg with a woman by his side. From his obituary, I knew his first wife's name was Ruth Irene (Cook), and that she'd died December 30, 1926, of scarlet fever.

Bud didn't recognize the woman, but he'd been adopted after Ruth had died. He did point out the pictures of Art with his second wife, Margaret. These were obviously pictures from the '40s and '50s.

The other woman had to be Ruth. One picture was of Ruth alone, standing shyly on a rock, wearing a typical 1920s flapper dress. Her pose suggested this was at the start of romance. There was innocent coquettishness in her eyes. Later pictures were of her and Art, both wearing wedding rings and standing in front of an unfamiliar building. There seemed to be a strain between husband and wife.

One of the earlier pictures captured a family picnic, the location unknown. Bud said Bonham Reservoir had been a favorite campsite of the family, but he wasn't sure if this was Bonham. In the pictures, J.B. Gesberg was in the forefront and Ruth, partially hidden, was next to him. They and a small crowd made of family and friends were gathered around a campfire. I think Art was taking the pictures since most of the subjects were slightly out of focus, except the face of his wife, which was crystal clear. Obviously, he only had eyes for her.

My pulse quickened when I saw another picnic picture taken the same day and it showed Ruth Gesberg about four or five months pregnant.

From the obits, I knew only one Gesberg son had brought forth offspring, that being Harold, the oldest. Bernice was born to Harold and his first wife, Ana, in 1921. Leslie, the second oldest, had married Elizabeth and adopted Bud at the age of five; Carl had been married for only ten years to Charlotte Young, producing no children, and Art, the youngest, had been married and widowed twice.

Art's obit said he'd moved to Pueblo and married Margaret Wilson, who passed away in 1958. Art moved back to Grand Junction in 1961 and died in 1975, with no children listed in his obituary. Yet, there was that picture . . . I thought I was on to something.

Bud Gesberg gave me those precious pictures and then suggested I contact the family of Betty Anderegg Brock, the stepdaughter of Harold Gesberg (his second wife, Wilma's, daughter), who'd just recently died. Ahna Brock, Betty's stepdaughter by marriage, met me at Betty's home and graciously let me borrow many of Betty and Wilma's mementos.

Reading through Wilma's journals and Betty's diaries, I got a much better image of life in Grand Junction from 1910 to 1940, and the Gesbergs. There were also many photographs, a lot from our own Dean Studios, including an original school picture of Dalton Trumbo. As a thank you to the Brocks, I arranged their pictures by date, some as early as 1894, and labeled them with names of those I knew well by that time.

A relative of the Brocks gave me Bernice Gesberg Miller's phone number. This was Harold's daughter, the only living blood relative of the Gesbergs. I knew from Harold's obituary that she'd lived in California way back when, but when I had searched the AOL white pages earlier for her name or her husband, Gorham, it brought no results. And there had been a long list of Bernice Millers when I'd used the Social Security Death Index. Therefore, I was very excited to finally contact Bernice Miller.

In her early eighties, Bernice still lives in California with her husband. I called her and we had the most delightful conversation about her family and the Fair Store. Bernice remembered so much about the running of the Fair, William Moyer, and her grandfather's role at the store. She even had a Fair Store doll that was given to her in the 1920s.

She didn't remember very much about Art after his wife, Ruth, had died of scarlet fever. She'd been only five but she had attended Ruth's funeral and remembers Art weeping. He was devastated, she said. He left Grand Junction soon after (in 1929 says his obituary), giving Bernice his and Ruth's dog, Peggy. Bernice didn't remember Ruth ever being pregnant in the four years she was married to Art, nor had she heard of a baby dying.

The next few decades, according to Bernice, Art rarely visited Grand Junction or his family until he moved back from

Pueblo in 1961. In the interim, his father, J.B., had died in 1933, and his mother, Agnes, in 1939.

I wanted to know what he'd done right after Ruth's death. Bernice had said he'd moved away, but she thought it was earlier than 1929. This was probably more correct, because in Grand Junction's city directories they didn't have Art listed from 1928 until the early 1960s. I knew at some time he'd moved to Pueblo. I would have to make a trip there to check the directories.

Until then, I did what I could online. A check with the 1930 Federal census didn't have Art Gesberg listed. Every other member of his family was there, but no Art. Where had he gone? There were no military or prison records, no Colorado addresses, either. The man simply dropped off the face of the earth.

Then came a most devastating day. It was May 21, 2003. I'd gone to the museum to find pictures of the Fair Store interior. I had a couple outside pictures, one taken around 1921 and the other after a renovation in 1930. Judy Prosser-Armstrong checked her files and found a 1921 picture similar to the one I had, except the employees were standing out front, and someone had been thoughtful enough to list their names. Among them was the name *Ruth Cook*, which I knew was Ruth's maiden name.

My joy turned to dismay when the face of Ruth Cook was not the face of the pregnant woman I thought was Art's wife! I'd been wrong all along!

The next day, Ben and I were heading to Colorado Springs for a Yanni concert. Originally, we'd planned to stop off in Pueblo to research Art and his second wife, Margaret's, life there. I had several pictures of Art and Margaret together, and one with Art and Margaret and another young couple. The young woman was a softer image of the pregnant woman I'd thought was Ruth. Maybe she was a relative.

And there was one of Art and "Ruth" taken in front of a building that wasn't in Grand Junction. We needed to check that out.

I'd looked forward to this trip, but now what was the use? I'd gotten the whole story wrong. Ben thought we should go anyway. You never knew. I barely enjoyed the lovely ride to Pueblo. I prayed a lot, and after prayer, I felt peace.

The first stop in Pueblo was its main library. I asked Ben to look up anything he could on the name Gesberg and I checked city directories starting at 1928. In 1932's directory, I finally found Art's name. And right next to his name was another. *Lillian M.*

Margaret had not been Art's second wife. She'd been his third!

In shock, I checked the 1933 directory and found Lillian's name again mentioned next to Art's. The 1934 and 1935 directories were missing. I asked for 1936, and boy was I surprised to see the name, *Margaret*, listed as Art's wife. What had happened to Lillian?

Ben had no luck with the name Gesberg other than Margaret's death notices. She'd died of a heart attack while dining at a restaurant, in 1958. No death record of a Lillian Gesberg.

We wrote down Art's work addresses and all home addresses until the 1950s, and then Ben and I got out a map and drove to them all. First thing I saw when we found the address of Art's first business, Silver State Oil Co, now a Mexican restaurant, was the building I'd been curious about in the background of the picture with Art and "Ruth." Some workers who were replacing the cement steps told us it had once been a church, but it was now a playhouse.

Across the street from that was where Lillian and Art had lived when they'd first come to Pueblo.

Given the evidence, Art and Lillian had to have gotten divorced. I knew it took approximately two years to get divorced back then. If Art married Margaret in 1936, then they had to have separated and filed for divorce around 1934.

Ben and I followed the map to the other residences and found the one where both Art and Margaret and the couple had stood together for a picture. That young couple must have been Lillian and her beau or new husband. Art and Margaret lived at this address in the early 1940s. I liked that there was so little animosity between Art and Lillian that they would visit and take a picture together.

I've been unable to find out what happened to Lillian. Her maiden name has not shown up anywhere, including a Colorado marriage certificate search. She and Art weren't married in Grand Junction, Pueblo, or Colorado. As of this writing, I'm still waiting for a divorce certificate search in Colorado.

If Colorado records are correct, Art and Lillian weren't married here. For a short time, Art lived elsewhere, met Lillian, got married to her, and sometime they moved back to Grand Junction where Lillian got pregnant. They probably lived with his parents in their five-bedroom home overlooking the Gunnison River. The picture of Lillian pregnant was before 1933, since J.B. died that year, and he looks pretty healthy in the picture. By studying the fashions, both in clothes and eyeglasses worn in the picture, I determined it was probably taken around the summer of 1928-29. Since neither he nor Lillian are mentioned in the 1930 census, it's possible they were in the process of moving (right after Our Darling's death?) and missed the census.

Yes, I'm sure Lillian was the mother of Our Darling and Art was the father. My theory is based solely on circumstantial evidence, but what is amazing is there hasn't been one thing to *disprove* my theory. In all the research I've done, nothing has pointed in another direction. As a matter of fact, it seemed like my steps had been guided all along.

Art Gesberg had been an emotional man. He'd been the sensitive brother, with gentle and kind eyes. He'd felt things deeply. I'd often wondered what would have driven him away from the place where his whole family lived — the place where he grew up and loved. In this town, he'd lost his beloved first wife, and then his only child. Had the pain been too great? Would a new start somewhere else help?

Wherever Art met Lillian, she must have brought happiness to him after the death of Ruth. And with the promise of a baby, the very symbol of new life, Art's sorrow must have diminished even more. With Our Darling's untimely death, his devastation was complete. Both Art and Lillian look sad, despite their smiles, in the picture taken on the corner of the Silver State Oil Company. I'm guessing this was taken within a couple of years of the baby's death.

Perhaps they'd tried to overcome their sorrow, perhaps even tried for another baby and failed. Our Darling had been a miracle baby in the first place, given the Gesberg brothers' rate of propagation. It must have been too much for their marriage to endure, for they eventually separated and divorced.

In 1936, Art married a thirty-something schoolteacher and remained happily married to her for twenty-two years. After Margaret's death, Art hung around Pueblo for three more years before moving back to Grand Junction. He and his brother, Carl, shared a home on Orchard Mesa. According to Bernice, Art started drinking heavily and did so until his death in 1975.

Shortly after Our Darling was reburied at Orchard Mesa Cemetery, May 11, 1972, a handpicked bouquet of flowers was laid across her grave. Art was known for growing beautiful roses.